MY WILDEST DATE

RAISED BY WOLVES BOOK 3

CASEY MORALES

WWW.AUTHORCASEYMORALES.COM

PREFACE

You're going to find this hard to believe, especially when you learn how gullible I was at twenty-two when this series began, but what you're about to read is a true story. Yes, I have changed names and places to protect the guilty, and embellished here and there, but the bones of the tale are true.

What can I say? I was a modern-day Gomer Pyle.

I was *that* preacher's kid. You know, the one who never knew he was supposed to be secretly rebellious and get away with a hidden wild side. Yeah, I missed that memo. I was the PK who was *actually* into being righteous and good—whatever that means these days.

I grew up in a kind, loving household, with three older sisters. The youngest was seven years older than me, so it was like being an only child with five parents.

Now, years later, I know that was the perfect setup for coming out later in life, but at the time, I had no clue. I was convinced I would one day have a beautiful wedding in a massive church with flowers and candles everywhere.

You're snickering. How rude.

Anyway, you get the picture. Good boy. Innocent. Completely clueless. And *definitely* straight. Did I mention that? I was straight, doggone it.

I firmly believed I'd made it through high school and college without meeting a single gay person. I was convinced, as was taught from the pulpit on Sundays, that all gays lived in California or New York. I was never clear on why those two particular states had become a haven for homosexual hedonism, but as long as I stayed away from those evil places, everything would be fine. Right?

Little did I know my best friend from fourth grade through high school was a screaming queen—and not the subtle basketball-playing gay who looked sideways at the other boys in the showers. Oh no. He was the chiffon-waving, *hey-gurl*-yelling signal fire that could be seen from space.

How was I supposed to know? Just because he was the drum major in the marching band—

And your snickering continues.

I see now that we are not going to have a serious,

adult conversation, so I may as well get on with the story.

I hope you laugh out loud, squirm a little, get a bit overheated, and maybe even shed a tear.

Aw, who am I kidding? I just want you to laugh, and drool over the steam. Isn't that what we're all here for anyway?

Good luck, dear reader. Enjoy the ride.

Oh crap.

I said *ride*.

1

PANCAKE BLISS

"Just breathe between sentences, okay?" Dwayne motioned for me to slow the word vomit spewing out of my mouth. His amused grin belied his annoyed tone and motherly palm.

"Sorry," I said, not sorry at all. "I guess you had to be there. It was the most incredible day I could ever imagine."

Thanksgiving was a couple weeks ago, and perky festive tunes rang throughout the diner. I'd just talked through Dwayne's coffee, pancakes and eggs without touching my own plate. He had practically licked his clean as Katie, our regular waitress, pried it from his bony fingers. They exchanged a wry glance before she shuffled off to her next table.

None of that mattered.

I walked Dwayne through the weekend with

Carter and the kids, ending with a Picasso-like portrait of Saturday's lawn-mowing, leaf-pile-tossing, picture-perfect day. Carter had had his older son, Cade, on his lap as they made meticulous lines in the grass with the riding mower. Carter was determined to get one last cut in before winter grabbed us by the, um, throat.

Meanwhile, I was responsible for watching three-year-old Christian. Not to be outdone by Carter's heroic, ride-on-my-lap dad trick, I had taken my little monster to the man-sized pile of leaves and tossed him in. The pile shook with his giggles. Before I knew it, we were both rolling around, tossing leaves at each other and crying with happy laughter.

That's when it happened.

I looked up from the flurry of tiny hands and fluttering leaves and time froze. It was as if someone had pressed a button on a magical camera and everything paused.

In that moment, I had *everything* I'd ever wanted.

I had a partner who loved me, two beautiful boys whose smiles filled my soul in ways I'd never experienced, and hope for an incredible future.

Despite his palm-waving, Dwayne couldn't quell my excitement.

I could see in the tiny, upturned lines around his eyes that mirrored his smile that he didn't want to either. He was happy for me. He was nearly twice my age, but he was my best friend, the one person in the world I could tell everything and know I would never be judged.

Um, okay, that's not exactly true. I knew I *would* be judged. It's what we gays do, isn't it? Our DNA requires it. It's science.

Anyway.

Dwayne's judgment wasn't snarky or self-interested. It was borne of genuine empathy and concern, like a brother or father—or true friend.

"You've been dating how long now?" he asked as he eyed me over the rim of his chipped coffee mug.

"Three months."

My alarms were starting to sound. Where was he going? Was there a lesson coming from the sensei that would sober my giddy mood?

He nodded sagely. "That's a good amount of time. Just guard yourself."

"What do you mean?" I hadn't intended to sound defensive, but there it was.

"I don't want to see you hurt. That's all."

"Hurt? Why would Carter hurt me?" I *really* didn't like this conversation anymore. Maybe his judgment was judgy, after all.

Dwayne set his mug down and leaned forward. "Michael, you've barely slept a night at your own place since you met him. Things have moved so fast I can barely keep up. I know it feels wonderful right now, but Carter's life has complications. That can change things over time."

"Complications?" Now I was totally defensive.

His palms flew up in a *don't shoot the messenger* motion.

"I'm happy for you, really. Just try to take things one day at a time, alright?"

I had no idea what he meant, but nodded as if Confucius himself had just granted his wisdom.

In my moment of Zen-like confusion, Katie's hand found my shoulder. She leaned over and whispered into my ear, "Sweetie, don't listen to him. It's wonderful seeing you so happy."

I reached up and gave her hand a squeeze and smiled up in thanks. Dwayne downed the last of his coffee, tossed his usually healthy tip on the table, and began scooting out of the booth. "Gotta run," he said. "I'll talk to you soon. Have fun with lover boy."

Now *that* I could do.

Maybe Dwayne's sensei abilities were spot-on after all.

WHERE DID SANTA GO?

The Christmas countdown clock was ticking loudly now. Eight days 'til Santa.

Christian and Cade couldn't talk about anything else. I'd helped Christian make his list, which consisted of more Matchbox cars, stuffed animals, and a Batman costume. Batman and Robin were his big brother's favorite cartoon characters on Saturday morning, so they were now his too. It was cute.

Cade was two years older than my charge, which made his list twice as long. I didn't even recognize some of the toys and games on his crumpled paper. He carried it everywhere he went, as if showing more adults what he wanted would make them more likely to appear. Carter tried prying it out of his hands once, but the fit that ensued convinced us both to leave list management to the little one.

The four of us piled into Carter's SUV and searched for the perfect tree, then hauled it home and spent another hour decorating it. I'd never been into the whole Christmas cheer thing, but the boys had won me over to Santa's side.

There's an inexplicable joy hanging tinsel with a three-year-old—and they get *so* excited as each ornament appears. His deep brown eyes widened when I handed him a plastic Rudolf, then he giggled when I flipped the hidden switch and the reindeer's nose blinked.

I looked up to find Carter lifting Cade so he could place decorations near the tree's top, smiles plastered on both their faces.

My heart felt like it would burst.

THAT NIGHT, DURING OUR THURSDAY NIGHT RITUAL OF snuggling on the couch watching an episode of *LA Law* (hey, it was the '90s, that show was amazing), our little men fell asleep an hour before their normal bedtime, exhausted from another day preparing for Santa. Carter paused the TIVO, and we carried them into their room and tucked them snugly under their covers. I leaned down to kiss Christian's forehead and felt a tiny finger trace my jaw. His eyes never opened, but a thin smile curled his lips.

I heard Carter clanking dishes in the kitchen and knew he was making our bedtime snack of cottage cheese and canned fruit. This was a delicacy I'd never experienced before meeting him, but now I couldn't go to sleep without it. I curled up on the couch to await my gourmet goblet of goodness.

The kitchen quieted.

I let a few minutes pass, then curiosity got the best of me, so I headed into the kitchen. Carter was sitting at the table, staring into his untouched fruit. A second bowl was made for me, sitting in front of the chair opposite his.

This was odd. We always sat beside each other, not opposite—and our nighttime snack was eaten in the den while watching TV.

As I sat and waited, my Spidey sense began to tingle—and not in the good way. Something significant was about to happen.

"Everything okay?" I ventured.

When he looked up, I knew my world was about to change. His eyes were rimmed red and a trickle flowed down one cheek.

"Carter, what's wrong?"

"I'm so sorry," was all he could get out before he choked on a sob.

I was kneeling by his chair in a flash, one hand on his arm, the other gently rubbing his back. "Hey. I'm right here. Whatever it is, we'll face it together."

That made his sobs grow.

"Her lawyer called," he muttered.

Now I was confused—and deeply concerned. "Lawyer? Whose lawyer?"

"Jen's." Jen was his ex-wife; the boys' mother.

My heart seized.

"Christian was so excited the other day." He sucked in a breath and locked eyes. "When I took them back to her place after their visit, he talked about it all week. Jen hadn't realized you were staying here on my weekends with the boys."

Another wave hit him, and he couldn't talk for a few minutes. I waited, having no idea what to say.

"You can't stay here anymore."

The room tilted.

My head swam.

"Oh. Well, um, that's okay, I guess. I'll just stay at my place when the boys are here. That's not a big deal."

It *was* a big deal, but they weren't my kids, I had no skin in this game. That's what I told myself, grasping for anything that would numb the pain blooming in the center of my chest, but it refused to be dulled.

He shook his head. "No, it's bigger than that. She's threatening to take me to court, to challenge our joint custody, if you sleep here one more night. Her lawyer said something about Tennessee judges not looking favorably on *gay influence* in situations like this."

Gay influence? What the hell was that? I understood the conservative approach to parenting—my own wolves had made sure of that—but I'd never been anything but supportive of Carter's decisions and was a positive influence on the boys. Carter and I never kissed in front of them, just to make sure stories couldn't get back to their mom.

"The lawyer said Cade told them about jumping on you while you were in the bed with me. He said you were naked."

"That's ridiculous." Now I *was* pissed. "I never got out from under the covers. The boys have never seen me less than fully clothed."

"I know, but the truth doesn't matter, only what they can make a judge believe." His head drooped. "I can't lose them, Michael. I can't lose my boys."

His hand was shaking as he took mine and kissed it. My last defense shattered with that simple act, and I began to cry with him. He dropped from his chair, pulled me down, and held me on the floor as we wept.

$$3$$

SHOCK AND AWE

"I don't know how long we sat there on his kitchen floor, holding each other and crying. It felt like all night. I kissed each of the kids on the forehead as they slept and haven't seen them since."

Katie's arms were a vise around my shoulders as they shuddered. She pressed my head into her shoulder, tears staining her white apron.

"Have you talked to Carter since?" Dwayne's voice was soft and soothing.

I wiped my face with a scratchy paper napkin and shook my head. "We talked on the phone last week. He said he didn't think he could do this anymore." I spat more than spoke that last part.

"Just like that?" Katie was indignant in my defense. Bless her.

I nodded. "Yeah, just like that. I can't blame him

though. If I had to choose—" A new round of sobs slammed into me at the thought of Christian and Cade, realizing I wouldn't see them at Christmas—and might never see them again.

ON CHRISTMAS EVE, THE PACK GATHERED AT MY parents' house.

A month earlier, as we'd gathered for Thanksgiving, I'd come out to my oldest sister, Nise, and told her about Carter. She'd been amazing, telling me she only cared that I was happy and with someone who loved me. I hadn't mentioned the boys. That would've been more than even the most understanding wolf could take.

Apparently, my mom, the unchallenged alpha in this pack, had seen us fogging the glass in my beloved Saturn and had grilled Nise about the conversation after I'd left. I never knew my mom had lived a secret life as a Soviet interrogator, but her skills at making people talk were unmatched. Combine that with her Pisces sixth sense and no secret was safe. Nise was no match for Comrade Nell. My most closely held secret was dragged out in the open for the whole family to see.

But here's the best part—I didn't know *any* of that

when I showed up for Christmas. The KGB hadn't sent a note.

Apparently, they liked surprises.

I strolled into the house, a pack of clothes slung over my shoulder, pillowcase filled with wrapped presents weighing down my other hand. The greeting I received was not filled with the festive cheer I'd expected

My mom and dad sat on one side of their round oak dining table. Nise glanced up from her seat opposite the inquisitors. There was something in her gaze I didn't recognize. I now know it was pity.

"Why don't you set your things down in the den and join us? We'd like to talk before the others get here." My father's voice was calm and welcoming, as if he was inviting me to eat dinner or grab a coffee. That unnerved me more than if he'd yelled.

As soon as my butt hit the wicker chair, Comrade Mama lobbed her first grenade. "Is there anything interesting you'd like to tell us?"

Oh, this was bad. She was opening with the *I'm not giving you any information* approach. I was well and truly screwed. Nise looked like she wanted to crawl under the table.

"Um, well, can you narrow it down a bit? Give me a topic?"

Mom's gaze was steel. "How about we start with

Pat—or should I call *him* Carter now?" She crossed her arms in triumph.

Shit.

As a great philosopher once said, "Resistance is futile." I decided to just go with the conversation, as if there was nothing unusual in talking about a boyfriend with my preacher dad and zealot mom—the ones I didn't know had learned I was gay while my back was turned.

"Sure. Okay. Carter is someone I was dating."

Mom spat her overly sweetened tea across the table. I looked up, brow quirked.

"Dating?" she hissed. "You call it dating now?"

Ah, I understood. She'd switched to the religious *gays don't belong in our world* card. I should've seen it coming.

Honestly, at the time, *I* was uncomfortable calling it dating. Everything still felt new and strange, but there really wasn't a better word, at least not that I could think of. She certainly didn't need to know about the canoodling that went on behind closed doors. That would've destroyed Christmas.

Rather than offer a sharp retort, I nodded and quietly said, "Yes, we dated. We went to dinner and movies. We watched TV and cooked. We did all the normal things you'd expect from two people getting to know each other."

Her gaze was hardening, so I decided to make a peace offering. "But you don't need to worry about Carter anymore. Things…ended."

I heard Nise suck in a breath. When I dared a look in her direction, she mouthed, "I'm sorry."

"Denise!" the all-seeing eye snapped, and Nise's head fell.

My dad finally leaned in.

In all my daydreams—and nightmares—about coming out to my parents, he was the one I feared would slam the door. He was the man who stood in the pulpit and talked about how being gay was an abomination, citing one example after another, where city walls and stones were the only solution to the *gay* problem. He didn't disappoint in his reticence on the issue, but he did surprise me with his calm, empathetic tone.

"Michael, we love you, no matter what," he said.

My throat caught. Was he—

"But, since Carter's no longer in your life, do you think it might be a good time to, I don't know, get some help?"

Help? What in the ever-loving gay hell was that supposed to mean?

My pulse raced, and I began to sweat. Without a word, Nise, my only ally, my lifeline, stood and scurried out of the room.

Whiskey Tango Foxtrot!

I looked up at my dad and thought his heart might be beating as loudly as mine. He looked even more uncomfortable than I felt. "Help? What do you mean?"

He glanced at my mom, but her icy glare remained fixed on me.

He sipped his tea, then carefully set his glass down, the gentle thud of Walmart's finest crystal hitting wood the only sound in the room.

"I found a place that…they help people…boys like you," he stammered, eyes dropping to his weathered hands, unwilling to meet my eyes.

I couldn't believe what I was hearing. My dad was suggesting I consider going to a reform school for gays? I'd heard stories on the news about them. Some used shock or drug therapy to help *fix* a gay person's brain, as if there was some faulty wiring that simply needed an adjustment. Most of the tales about such places were horrific, and the only successes I'd heard of came from the guys who'd managed to hook up while there, sometimes with their instructors (or whatever you call them).

Let's go with Daddies.

"I know someone who went through a program like this. He's married now." My dad's voice was more plea than statement. He was miserable suggesting this, but he also sounded helpless. As confident as my mom's gaze appeared, I knew she was scared of losing me, whether to gayness or my own obstinance. Now my dad looked lost and alone.

Was he just as confused dealing with my feelings as I had been?

Then a realization struck. I'd had time to think through my feelings. It had been a few years since my first experience. While I was nowhere near confident in my new self, I wasn't looking in that mirror for the first time either.

My parents, on the other hand, had just learned everything. There were layers of complexity in their feelings in that moment.

First, in their eyes, the son they thought they knew —the one they raised to follow my dad into the pulpit —no longer existed. Sure, I was sitting right there. But in that moment, their eyes told me they were seeing *a stranger* sitting across that table. They had no idea who I was. Everything they thought they knew had turned upside down when Nise let the truth of Carter slip.

They weren't just afraid for my soul; they were mourning the death of a child they knew and loved.

They were also mourning the loss of a future they'd dreamed about since holding me as their newborn son—their *only* son. They'd dreamed of a wedding, followed by grandchildren. They'd dreamed of a life like they'd enjoyed, except this time with the freedom to spoil that comes with the title grand-what-ever. None of that would happen now. I would never father children, grand or otherwise. While I had nieces and nephews, in my dad's paternalistic view, *his line* would end with me.

As angry as I was at the suggestion I needed help, I couldn't stop myself from feeling a deep empathy for their struggle. Their religious beliefs weren't an act. They weren't some suits they donned on Sundays to impress the neighbors. Their beliefs were the core of their beings. While our views definitely differed, I still respected theirs. They were sincere, good people, and I loved them both. Seeing their pain added to my own.

Until my mother spoke again. "You know you can never bring a *man* into our home. We could never allow that."

So much for the goodwill gesture.

I stood, nearly knocking my chair over as it slid back. "Keep telling me I need help and you'll be lucky if I bring *myself* back into this house, much less anyone else." I was proud of that line.

Then I turned to my dad, venom in my voice. "And how dare you. I just lost someone I loved. I came here, *hurting*, feeling more alone than at any time in my life, and the first thing you suggest is I enjoy the warm embrace of electroshock therapy? Nice one, Dad."

His head fell and any pride I might've had in that snappy retort dropped like a stone in my gut.

I grabbed the pack with my clothes and stormed out of the kitchen to the solitude of my old bedroom, leaving a pair of stunned and hurt parents staring at the chair that once held their son.

4
____

HO, HO, HO

The rest of the pack arrived within hours.

Tension flashed between the adults like lightning, but we kept everything in check for the kids, determined to let them be children and enjoy their holiday, regardless of whatever Grinch-like havoc I might've wrought.

Family tradition dictated the opening of exchanged presents on Christmas Eve, followed by the opening of Santa's deliveries at some ungodly hour on Christmas morning. The festivities were capped with a glutenous meal around two o'clock on Christmas Day. My dad usually found his La-Z-Boy and passed out within thirty minutes of his fork's final clank, but not this year. I felt his hand on my shoulder and knew there would be another *talk*.

I sighed. Nise, who was sitting beside me, grabbed my hand under the table and gave me a supportive squeeze. Then I rose to face the executioner.

It was freezing outside, so my dad suggested we take a drive down to our gas-station-adjacent office. If you missed that part, yes, we rented space attached to a gas station for our family wholesale drug business my dad ran when he wasn't doing the part-time preacher thing. It wasn't big, nor was it glamorous, but it was close to their house and was all we needed. I sat in my spinny office chair. He grabbed a folding chair and sat with his knees almost touching mine.

This can't be good.

He'd called this meeting, so I kept quiet as a long moment passed and he gathered his thoughts. He was clearly struggling, which was not normal for the always-ready-to-speak preacher man.

"Michael, I want to say…I mean, after yesterday in the kitchen…well, that wasn't…"

Wow, he's really flummoxed.

"I just want to say I'm sorry."

Shit. That wasn't the sermon listed on the program.

"I didn't realize how much he…I mean, Carter… meant to you. If I'd known, I never would've suggested any of those things. I know I shouldn't have anyway, but I really wouldn't have if I'd known." He put his head in his hands, and I thought he might actually cry. I'd only ever seen him cry twice: at his mother's funeral, and as he held my mother at her father's funeral. He'd actually shed more tears comforting her than he had allowed himself for his own loss. He was such a good man in that way.

He looked up. A tear had escaped. His voice shook when he continued. "You're more important to me than *anything* in this world. You know that, don't you? I'm *so* sorry you're hurting. We don't have to talk about anything else. Just tell me how you're doing. Please. Let me help you."

Dammit. I lost my shit right there in our office.

My dad was so sincere, so heartfelt. I fell into his arms and became a five-year-old boy seeking shelter and safety in his father's embrace. All the grief from losing Carter, even more from losing my connection to the boys, poured out of me. Between sobs, I told him how hurt I was, how much I'd thought Carter was *the one*. I know it hurt him to hear me refer to another man that way, but he held me tighter, and his tears fell with my own.

Now, don't get crazy, he wasn't accepting me being gay or giving up hope I might return to the fold one day, but he was putting our relationship as father and son above everything else. This man I'd expected to cast me out of the pack—to stone me outside our city walls—chose to hold me closer when the darkness came.

However long I live, I may never experience a more beautiful moment.

5

AOL INCHES DON'T COUNT

The holiday encounter with the pack had taken place over the weekend, so I got back to my apartment Sunday night, the day after Christmas Day.

For those of us trapped within the borders of our own land, the day after Christmas is known as Boxing Day to the rest of the world. Modern thought suggests it's the day to *box up* everything from Christmas, though the origin of the day was more likely related to servants or workers on estates being given gifts (in boxes) the day following the land-owning family's celebration. Either way, like many traditions that began with the best intentions, it turned into a giant commercial opportunity for retailers to offer crazy sales and handle lame gift returns.

Why am I giving you a history lesson on Boxing

Day? I have no clue. I just remember that's the day I escaped the pack.

Stop distracting me.

My roommate Peter had traveled to spend Christmas with his family, so I had the apartment to myself until New Year's Day when he returned. I was glad. A week to myself would let me process everything that had happened over Christmas.

The morning after his return, I walked my bleary-eyed self into the kitchen and was greeted by Peter, who was sitting shirtless on a bar stool eating Frosty Pebbles.

Yes, Peter was a personal trainer with abs on his toes, but he loved his sugary goodness. He could've eaten every Frosty Pebble ever made and still look like a Greek statue. It was infuriating—but not the worst sight to see first thing in the morning.

"You don't look mopey today. That's an improvement."

He'd been trying to shake me out of my funk for months, but, because I was a total wuss and hadn't come out to him yet, he still believed the Pat story and thought I'd been dumped by a Hooters waitress.

Hey! Stop giggling. If I'm going to date a ficti-tious woman, she's going to have *huge* tatas and tiny shorts. That's just how I roll.

"Guess time does heal."

He eyed me, but kept munching. "Anything you want to share?"

I nearly dropped my coffee mug. What did he mean by that? Had he heard something? Had my mother secretly conspired with him to grill me for information? He didn't know my family. How could he know Pat wasn't real? That's what he was saying, right?

I tried not to freak out. "Uh, I don't know. Like what?"

He finished his overstuffed mouthful and set his bowl down. It took forever for him to stop chewing. I flinched as he tossed his spoon against the empty ceramic with a *clank*. Why was I suddenly so nervous?

"So, two things. You should probably sit down."

I sat, feeling like the kid waiting outside the principal's office.

Peter stood and leaned over the counter. I couldn't help admiring how his arms flexed, despite the tsunami I sensed coming.

"First, I've known Pat wasn't real for months. I get why you never told me, but you should know you can tell me anything. I don't care that you're gay, only that you're my brother."

I swallowed hard.

"Second, and this is the part you may not like, I'm moving out."

My head snapped up. "What? You're—"

"Actually, it's more than that. I'm joining the navy. The recruiter said he could get me into the SEAL program—at least, get me into the tryouts for it. I have to earn my way in from there."

My mouth closed, but my eyebrows shot to the ceiling. "SEALs? Really? But you're…*a model.*"

I didn't mean for that last part to sound so judgy, but there it was.

He laughed. "Crazy, isn't it? My dad was a SEAL. My uncle was a SEAL. It's something I've always wanted to do, but never thought I could. The program's intense and most guys fail out."

My head was spinning. "Wow. SEALs. I don't even know what to say. That's awesome…and totally sucks. I don't want to lose you."

He cocked his head like a confused German shepherd.

"I mean, you're a good roommate and all. I'll hate to see you go."

He reached across and mussed my hair. Was I twelve? What was that? "I'll miss you too." He turned to walk toward his bedroom. "I leave tomorrow. If you want to tell me about Carter before I go, now's the time."

Holy shit. He even knew Carter's name.

I watched him vanish down the hallway, speechless for the third time before my first full cup of coffee. This was going to be a really weird day. I'd have to start getting used to the idea of living alone. I wasn't glad about that.

Peter and I had been roommates for a couple of years. His straight hotness might've been frustrating—and an utter waste of a smokin' hot guy with gay rockstar potential—but he was a great roomie. We lived separate lives, but enjoyed each other's company when our paths converged at home. We respected each other's space, shared the bills, and he was a great coach at the gym. I hated him for that last part some days, but he was largely responsible for my burgeoning physique, and that felt amazing.

Peter had taken a scrawny, scared guy and dragged him into the deep end where the muscle heads swam, somewhere he never would've ventured on his own. He showed that guy it was okay to be new and to struggle, that others had been there and would help. He helped him gain confidence he'd never known.

He helped *me* gain that confidence. I was going to miss him.

I flopped on the couch, more miserable than before. The goal had been to get home and cheer up by the time Peter returned. Nice work.

Something shiny caught my eye on the kitchen counter, so I hopped up to investigate. It was one of those magical discs that granted one thousand free hours of internet access—and it didn't come with a *for new subscribers only* label, which meant I could add a thousand freebies to my account. My mood suddenly shifted as I raced into my room, disc in hand.

A couple minutes and a dozen beep-bops later, a warm voice welcomed me to the World Wide Web. I checked my inbox. Nothing but coupons from Crate and Barrel and several emails bequeathing me an estate in Nigeria and Slovakia. How could there be so many princes out there I'd never heard of—and how did they all know my email address?

Annoyed by my lack of popularity, and still smarting from Christmas and Peter's pending departure, I turned to the only therapist I'd ever known, America Online Chat Rooms.

For those born after the glory that was the '80s, let me explain. Chat rooms were the very first online meeting places. They came in every variety and flavor, much like the people who entered them. For example, one might be interested in gardening. There were probably a thousand different rooms, with titles like *Green Thumbs in Indiana* or *Horticulture Rocks!* Yes, some of the names were lame, but you get the idea.

Now, forget plants.

If there were a thousand rooms for finding gardening tips, there were ten thousand for finding gardeners, and I'm not talking about the spade-wielding kind. These were rooms for meeting and talking with other men or women looking to date.

Yes, *date*—that's what they were looking for. Do you know what a euphemism is?

Anyway.

For our purposes, let's narrow the conversation to any room with a title containing the designation *M4M*, the universal label for men looking for other men. These were the gay rooms where good Christian boys sought other good Christian boys—

Wait, you *believed* that?

Most of the men chatting their lives away in *M4M* rooms were looking to meet other men. I'll be generous and say *some* of them wanted to get to know other guys, maybe have coffee or see a movie. You know, go on a date?

Bah! Most of the men online wanted one thing— and it wasn't the Crate and Barrel coupon.

The rooms with more aggressive appellations, such as *M4MNow!*, suggested those seeking dates would be better served elsewhere. The guys in this club had their own members primed and ready—*now!*

I'm not sure which bucket I fell into in that

moment. I'd never been one for casual sex. Then again, I'd thought I was straight most of my life. Not having sex with women was easy. Now that Little Michael was pointed in the right direction, resisting the urge was getting much harder.

Yes, I said harder. Stop that.

I knew my ultimate goal was to find someone special, to get to know him and build a life together. My time with Carter, however brief it might've been, had crystalized that dream in my mind. When it worked, it was beautiful. That's what I wanted.

But at the moment, I didn't have a Carter. I was a free agent.

I entered the benignly named *NashvilleM4M* room. There were twenty-two guys on the menu…I mean, in the directory. I clicked on the first screen name, Chad824. His profile was sparse, but said he liked reading, cooking, and gardening.

What was it with gardening onlinc?

Anyway, Chad824 had committed the ultimate AOL-profile party foul. He'd left any description of his physical attributes out. To any self-respecting, judgy gay, that ruled him right out.

Next.

I clicked on MuscleBrad. He sounded tasty—I mean, educated.

There was only one line in his profile. It read:

GWM, 34, 6'1, 31w, Brown/Blue, 16a, 8cThick—if online, looking—must have pix.

Yes, kids, this was how a profile was *supposed* to work. Brad was a gay white male, kinda tall with a sexy waistline. He had brown hair and blue eyes, bulging arms, and an even nicer bulge down below. Apparently, he thought so much of his bulge that he specified its impressive girth.

Here's another fun fact for the class: the term *AOL inches* was born from these stats. What if Brad, muscle-bound though he may be, was only packing six inches of, um, bulge? Surely, someone wouldn't lie about such a vital value, would they? Come to think of it, who even measures their member? Isn't that weird in itself? Anyway, AOL inches was the inside gay joke referring to a guy's real length versus his AOL profile's stated length.

The little *c* next to the eight was confusing to me at first. I had guessed it was a religious abbreviation, maybe Catholic? Alas, dear friends, that's *not* what that stood for, though some might infer which religion a boy belonged to (or didn't belong to) by the letter's presence.

Think scissors. Got it?

Brad was hunting a hookup, and was experienced enough online to only meet guys who could swap pictures. No, there was nowhere to upload a photo onto a profile back then. You had to actually talk to someone and agree to exchange pictures via email. AOL was great in some ways. That wasn't one of them.

I wasn't really looking for sex, but Brad sounded like a good Christian boy. I sent him an instant message (IM for you heathens): *Hey.*

Yeah, I was a literary genius.

While I waited for Brad to reply, I clicked on the next few profiles. Most had the obligatory line with stats, some contained lengthy paragraphs describing that person's ideal match. Others spent more time describing what they *weren't* looking for. Either way, it was fun to meet more people, safe in the anonymity of my own apartment, without having to go to a smoky bar.

After two hours of my magical thousand-hour freebie, I had eleven IM windows open and blinking rapidly.

Holy Mavis Beacon, Batman. I needed typing lessons. IMs moved fast—*really* fast. Just when you started one conversation, three more windows would pop up with prospective candidates seeking an inter-view—I mean, guys saying hello. If you got stuck chatting with one dude too long, others would start getting annoyed at your delayed response and either exit the IM or send a snarky message. Either way, if that happened, your odds with that particular applicant would decrease.

My fingers had never flown so fast.

And then I committed an AOL mortal sin: I sent a reply to the wrong guy.

The guy I was chatting with about his golden retrievers had a similar screen name to another dude who wanted me to lick his Weimaraner. I was really starting to like talking with Retriever29, but he didn't appreciate me asking whether his weeny dog was cut or not. He logged off in a huff.

In that moment, I had a gay epiphany.

I needed a system, some method of taking notes and cataloging the guys I chatted with. I opened a profile and hit Control-P. What spat out of my printer was a jumbled mess of a dude's profile, but it was workable, and there was enough white space for taking notes.

When my wall clock chimed eleven, I blinked the monitor haze from my eyes and stretched my back. I had somehow spent an entire day in chat rooms, and I wasn't even sorry—it had been exactly what I needed. I looked at my stack of printed profiles. Midway through the evening's adventure, I'd figured out how to copy and paste a photo onto the profile before hitting the print button, thus creating a more complete dossier. Dozens of guys smiled up at me, most shirtless, some showing their *very* happy Catholic wiener dogs.

Profiles of hot guys got a star or two. If the conversation was good, they got another star. If they were hot *and* could hold down a chat, their stars were circled.

I was an organized, AOL-loving…never mind. You get the idea.

As I hit the power button and listened to the whirring of the hard drive cease for the night, I laughed at myself. I knew it was silly and probably crazy, but I felt good again. There were so many guys out there, even in sleepy Nashville, surely one of them would be cool and want me.

For the first time since Carter had kicked me to the curb, I felt a twinge of hope.

Thank you, America Online. You're an *amazing* therapist.

6

THE BIG GAY DIAMOND

Did you know there are groups for virtually any activity or interest in the gay world? And not just on AOL, in real life?

Last night, while trolling the chat rooms like a good Christian boy, I'd found a room titled *GayMen4Chess*. My initial reaction was curiosity at how they'd misspelled the word *chest*, then I realized they meant the board game. Holy cow. It was a group of gay nerds who'd get together just to play chess.

Who knew?

My scrolling intensified and, besides the Kasparov Rainbow Club, there were groups for gay gardening (had to mention that one), gay travel, former military gays, service industry gays, and gays into drag. I suspect that last one was redundant.

There was even a group for gay couples looking

for other couples *FOR FRIENDS ONLY.* I thought it was funny how they put that last bit in all caps to ensure everyone knew they weren't there to hook up. Just for fun, I stuck my nose in and chatted with a few lovely gents. Two of the couples talked about their dogs and how they wanted to decorate their homes, but the third asked for my stats and pics right out of the gate.

Yeah, they wanted a threesome. I'd learned all about those in a movie a while back.

I clicked out of that room pretty quickly (although I did print the profile of one couple who seemed nice). No, it wasn't the throuple-seekers. Give me *some* credit.

Among the groups, I discovered Nashville had a gay softball league. I was blown away. Not too long ago, I didn't know another gay man existed near me. Now AOL was telling me there was a whole league packed full of softball-loving queens?

I jumped all over that shit. My email zipped out faster than a fart at Taco Bell.

Sorry, I know you love a sloppy Nacho Bell Grande. Who doesn't?

Five minutes flew by and my PC cried out, "You've got mail." I clicked the envelope of joy to find an email from the commissioner of the softball league. Indeed, they were accepting new players—and there was a tryout this weekend.

The gay gods were smiling on me again. And the congregation said, "Let there be rainbows and unicorns. Amen."

This was exciting. I loved playing most sports, and softball sounded like a fun way to get to know more guys, make some friends, and who knows what else? Add that to a Friday night social volleyball group I read about, and I might actually have a social life before it was all over.

Again, AOL's therapeutic skills were unparalleled. I was now in my first achy-cheek-smiling good mood since Christmas.

***

SATURDAY ARRIVED, AND ANTICIPATION BUBBLED inside me as I strode from my car to the dusty field. There were a few guys warming up, tossing balls back and forth, but most of the gaggle was gathered around the chorus-riser stands behind the home team's dugout.

I slowed my approach to appraise the competition.

The warmer-uppers looked decent, except for one poor dude who couldn't throw for shit. He made it look like an Olympic javelin toss as the ball either sailed miles over the receiver's head or flopped to the ground a foot in front of him. The guy playing catch with him closed the gap between them, grabbed the ball from the ground, and gave some sage coaching advice I wasn't sure would make any difference. I guessed some guys were here more for the social than competitive aspect.

Shifting my attention, I saw that most of the gaggle was unremarkable, dressed in T-shirts and shorts, some limbering up their gloves or swinging bats.

One guy wore a pink tutu. He was about six feet tall, barrel-chested, with a belly that stuck out like Santa and a bushy beard to match. From a distance, I could see wiry black hair clawing its way out of his shirt—the front *and* the back.

Holy Wookiee, Luke. We have ourselves a hairy fairy.

I later learned there was a *whole team* of guys who looked and dressed exactly like our dear Mr. Tutu. From my extensive academic research on the well-known hub of knowledge, AOL, I'd also learned that gays used animal names as descriptors. Guys with big bellies and pelts sprouting out of their pores were called *bears*. I did not, however, learn what one called a bear in a tutu. I made a mental note to research that one later.

"Michael?" a voice called out from the trees beyond the gaggle.

I craned my neck to find a blond guy in his midtwenties waving his hand above his head. He was practically hopping up and down to get my attention. I squinted, but couldn't place him. The social pressure of being called by name in front of a bunch of new guys pulled me to him like a magnet. When I got within reach, his arms flew outward and pulled me into a tight hug.

Whoever he was, he felt good—hard chest, strong arms, good hugger.

"You have no idea who I am, do you?" he said, grinning as he pulled back from the embrace. "It's okay. I'm better with matching profiles to real-life faces than most. I'm Scott, of *Scott and Jay*. We chatted last night."

"Oh!" I said, rapidly sifting through the printed pages in my mind. One with three stars in a bold circle flashed to the fore. "I remember now. You're the couple that lives downtown near Second Avenue, right?"

Scott beamed at being remembered, then took a step back and looked me up and down like I was a slab of beef in a butcher shop. "You need new pictures. Damn."

"Uh, is that a good thing?"

"Sure is. Jay's going to lose his mind when he sees you. He's out there trying to help that poor kid with throwing dyslexia." He pointed to the pair I'd noticed earlier.

"Throwing dyslexia?"

"That's what we call it when the ball goes opposite to where the thrower intends—*every time*." He laughed. "This must be your first time with the league. What level are you playing?"

Huh. They had levels. "I don't know. I played Little League baseball, but never softball on a team."

He examined me again and squeezed my bicep. I wasn't sure that was a necessary part of tryouts, but it *was* a gay league. What did I know? "Well, you look athletic. Come warm up with me, and we'll see how you do."

It took a minute to remember to keep my glove on the ground when fielding, but the mechanics came back quickly. Scott and I warmed up for ten minutes before a tall guy in a bright-orange cap walked out and blew a whistle. Those of us warming up gathered round and waited as the others took their time wrapping up conversations. They moved as one, a group giggle flowing in the wake of the gaggle.

Scott strode up to stand beside Jay. Like Scott, Jay was fit. He wore a white tank top, showing off taut arms and rounded shoulders. Scott motioned toward me with his eyes, and Jay scanned me like a copier, then looked back at his partner. He whispered something I couldn't hear, and they both grinned and nodded.

What had I gotten myself into?

We were divided into three groups: new players with throwing dyslexia, guys who had some basic hand–eye coordination, and skilled players who either played high school or college baseball. I stood with the middle group, a little annoyed that my prowess had been underrated. After another hour of fielding drills and batting practice, I discovered I had been accurately pigeonholed, because those higher-level players were the real deal. Their throws zipped across the field without a hint of an arc, and their batters hit more balls over the fence than inside the park.

Jay and Scott were placed with the experienced players. Scott was good, but Jay was ridiculous. I'd later learn he played baseball at Vanderbilt, which explained why every ball he struck landed in the parking lot well beyond the fence. He was a softball-slamming beast.

At the end of practice, Whistle Dude walked around and thanked each new player for trying out, and asked if they wanted to continue playing with a team. Those who answered affirmatively would be matched up with a team later in the week, and a follow-up email would be sent informing each player of their new assignment.

When Whistle got to me, he said, "Scott tells me you're pretty good. The Shooters need a pitcher. Think you could learn that position?"

He said that with a straight face, so I left the double entendre on the field. Man, that was a hard one to pass up. "Sure. That gets me in every play. I like it."

"Good." He scribbled something on his clipboard, nodded once, then moved on to his next victim.

I turned to leave, but was stopped by a hand on my shoulder. "I hear you just got signed up to pitch. Ever done that before?" The gleam in Scott's eye told me he had left no entendre on the field, double or otherwise.

I tried playing it straight. "No, never have. Should be fun."

Jay strolled up then and asked, "What should be fun? Are you coming over?"

"What—"

Scott chuckled at my wide eyes, then turned to Jay. "I haven't asked him yet. We were talking pitching…I mean, softball."

"I bet you were," Jay said with an eye roll before turning back to me. "Come have dinner at our place.

You seem like a nice guy, and we're trying to add to our friend list."

I cocked my head. "You guys need more friends? I find that hard to believe."

"You might be surprised. The minute you get a boyfriend, half the gay world thinks you're dead. The other half just wants to get in your partner's pants." Scott grinned at Jay. "I can't really blame them for that though, can I? Look at him. Who wouldn't want that?"

Jay snorted and tried to play it off, but I could see a blush forming in his cheeks. They were adorable together. There was an intimacy to their banter, a familiarity.

"So, dinner?" Jay dodged his blushing issue.

"Sure, sounds good."

We exchanged phone numbers, and Jay scribbled their address on the back of a softball flier. I waved as I drove out of the parking lot, completely missing the mischievous grins on both their faces.

7

BARBECUE AND FLUFF BALLS

I only got lost once on the way to Scott and Jay's house. The streets of downtown Nashville made my brain hurt; add in my terrible sense of direction, and one wrong turn was actually a victory.

Nashville's downtown was an odd jumble of short red-brick buildings dating back a hundred years or more, and shiny new skyscrapers. You might walk past the Ryman Auditorium where the Grand Ole Opry recorded its show for decades, then enter the lobby of the city's tallest tower, like the Bat Building, only a block or two away. The Bat Building was Bell-South's new headquarters. It wasn't actually named the Bat Building, but that's what everyone called in thanks to the odd glass and girder protrusions on its top that looked like Batman's ears.

There was an odd beauty in the tightly packed juxtaposition of old and new.

The guys lived just across the Cumberland River, almost within sight of historic Second Avenue. Yes, that's the same Second Avenue where the Wildhorse Saloon hosted a performance by my one-time obsession, Jason. I thought about that night briefly as I passed the multi-story bar. Why had I been so taken with him back then?

Jason had joined Dwayne and me for lunch a few times over the past few months. He was still hot, but now that I knew him, I was glad he wasn't looking for anything.

Let's call that a healthy miss.

I crossed the brackish waters of the Cumberland, and the quality of the real estate took a quick nose-dive. Tattered public housing rose to my right, while houses barely holding themselves together sprawled to my left. I tried to keep the sinking feeling now churning in my gut at bay, but it was determined to make this an uncomfortable drive.

Three left turns, two gas stations, and one liquor store with a shattered window later, I reached the sign for Pierce Avenue, the dead-end street where the boys lived. The first house I passed had an old refrigerator on the front porch. The fridge matched the rusty white car in the driveway, though the cinder blocks holding the car up didn't quite fit the rusted metal motif.

My family was never wealthy, and I had nothing against folks who struggled financially, but this was starting to make me nervous. Where the hell was I going?

The third house on Pierce towered over the others, a new two-story construction that looked like something off the cover of a real estate magazine. To either side of this majestic home were more houses with appliances as yard art. The yards themselves had less grass than the dusty infield at softball practice.

I finally reached the end of the street and looked up to find another two-story newbie. It was stunning. Most of the exterior was red brick, and each floor had its own deck that wrapped around the entire structure. Even the driveway looked freshly laid, its pearly white concrete barely showing signs of recent rain, much less wear. I double-checked the softball flier and confirmed the 243 on the door was my destination.

The knot in my gut relaxed as I walked up the driveway and Scott appeared in the open doorway. He wore a tall, puffy chef's hat and a broad smile. As I drew closer, he waved a wooden spoon and called out, "Come on in. I need to take the beans off the heat."

The sound of barking dogs grew louder, then abruptly stopped as the guardians of the castle peered out the open door, daring me to enter. I'm not sure what breed they were, something small, puffy, and white. The moment I leaned down, all three attacked my hand with warm, slobbery tongues.

"Wow. They don't like *anybody*." I looked up as Jay descended the wooden stairs.

I grinned and tried to reply, but words eluded me. The last time I saw Jay, he was wearing baggy baseball pants covered in dirt. Now, slightly above my eye level, sheer, tight-fitting light-blue shorts clung to every curve—and his curve was *huge*. I was pretty sure he wasn't wearing underwear by the swing on his porch. I really loved swings.

I swallowed the lump that sprung out of nowhere and threw my eyes back down toward the dogs, desperate not to look at the *taken* dude's package.

He chuckled, then turned. "Come on in. Scott's just about got dinner ready. Hope you like barbecue chicken and baked beans."

"Sounds great."

The fluff balls had apparently decided I was part of their pack and surrounded me as I followed the sound of clanking pots and utensils. The house was an interesting mix of log cabin and postmodern minimalist.

What am I saying? I don't know anything about architecture.

The walls were like a log cabin, where the wood had been flattened and polished to a sheen. The gooey stuff that held the logs together was visible, but sealed within the wood's clear coating. It was beautiful; I'd never seen anything like it. As I passed the den, I took a good look at the ceiling; white, with an intricate pattern of massive beams made of the same rich wood as the walls, giving the open floor plan a sense of height and rustic elegance. Long, puffy leather couches created a seating area around a large-screen television. It was warm outside, but the guys had lit a fire in the fireplace anyway.

There were photos everywhere—standing on tables, propped up against books in tall niches, and hung on every wall. Images of varying sizes told the story of Jay and Scott on a cruise ship, riding horses on a mountain path—and a *whole* lot more. In a number of the pictures, the boys were posing on various beaches wearing only speedos. I leaned in close to one photo and…

Sweet Chicken of the Sea, Jay's free-flopping curve looked even *bigger* in a banana hammock.

I turned and led the pack from their den of iniquity, finally reaching the kitchen. Scott was standing at the stove ladling beans into a serving dish. Jay was nuzzled up behind him, sneaking kisses on his neck. I paused, taking them in.

Set aside how beautiful each of them was in their own right—they were fit, muscular, sexy guys in the prime of life—but that wasn't what made me stare. It was the tenderness of the moment, the gentle kiss Jay pressed against Scott's neck, and the way Scott leaned back into his lover's touch. There was something so simple, so honest, in that gesture.

Scott must've felt me staring, because he looked up, winked, then shooed Jay away with his wooden spoon. "Go on now, the table isn't going to set itself." Scott turned to me and issued more orders. "You, come here. Help me put these dishes out."

And just like that, I realized Scott was the mother of the pack.

BEFORE WE DOVE INTO THE MEAL, SCOTT DOVE INTO conversation, asking everything he could about my past, present, and future. It felt a little like a job interview, but I secretly enjoyed the attention. I wasn't used to guys wanting to know all that stuff.

Jay finally rescued me. "I'm going to starve if you keep asking Michael questions. Let's eat."

Jay was dad. Got it.

Dinner was delicious. How can you not love barbecue? Scott used canned baked beans, but added so many spices and herbs they were barely recognizable from the original—and they were outstanding. Scott drank white wine, while Jay had beer. They gave each other a look I didn't quite follow when I asked for a Coke.

What is it about me asking for Coke that makes men grin?

The guys were as free with their own information as they had been with questions. Jay spoke like an online profile. "I grew up in Knoxville with my parents and three brothers, am a diehard Tennessee Vols fan, and work for a landscaping company. Scott and I met in college. He's the only man I've ever dated. We've been together for eight years, ten if you count freshman and sophomore years when we fucked but claimed we were straight and it was just a college phase."

They shared a grin and laughed in unison. Jesus, they were like the same person sometimes.

I eyed Jay's golden tan. As an Irishman, I'd always envied those with more than pasty pigments. I'd tried tanning oils, creams, even tanning beds, but nothing worked. The best I could do was make a few patches of freckles merge and pretend it was a tan. Melanin was repelled by my near-translucence.

Snapping out of my skin-tone envy, I turned to

Scott. "What about you? Was Jay your first and only?"

"Oh hell no. He was a slut," Jay barked.

Scott grabbed a fork and pretended to toss it at him from across the table, grinning the whole time.

"I was *very* friendly in college, thank you very much," he said dramatically. "I studied nursing, and work at Baptist Hospital now."

"What kind of nurse are you? I mean, where do you work in the hospital?" I asked.

"I work in the NICU, taking care of babies."

I tried not to swoon at the idea of sexy Scott holding a newborn, but it was the *perfect* profession for him. In the short time I'd known him, he'd impressed me with how he took care of everyone around him. He did it at the softball field, and he clearly took care of the pack here in his home.

It didn't hurt that he was a hardy Midwestern boy from Iowa.

He saw my awed expression and joked, "I was raised with good morals, muscles, and mothers."

I quirked my brow at that last statement, completely lost. Jay laughed and leaned over like he was telling me a secret. "He was raised by a pair of *lesbians*." He slithered out the last word as if he was a snake.

Oh. I think my mouth actually made that O shape.

I'd never heard of such a thing. My brain immediately tried to process the biology of his birth and came up empty.

Scott and Jay each barked a laugh, then Scott saved my impending aneurysm. "I was adopted when I was six months old. My birth mom was a drug addict who died in childbirth. If it weren't for two loving women coming to my rescue, I don't know where I'd be now."

I wanted to smile to show I understood, but the heartbreak of his birth held my pained expression in place—to lose his mother before he could know her.

Scott smiled. "It's all good. My moms are the best. They taught me everything I know about being a man and taking care of my own family."

I'd need to consult the Oracle of AOL for answers later. Women teaching a boy how to be a man puzzled my preacher's kid's mind.

Jay stood and started grabbing dirty plates. "Why don't we clean up, then we can watch a movie or something."

A movie. Or something? This sounded vaguely familiar.

We all moved to the kitchen, and I chided myself for making a naughty assumption. These guys were a couple. From what I could see, they were just about the happiest, most loving pair of dudes you'd ever meet.

What was I thinking?

And then Jay spoke. "I think we should get in the hot tub instead of watching a movie."

I almost dropped the glass I was washing. Hot tub?

"That's a *great* idea, babe. I'm still sore from softball, and it's so nice out tonight," Scott said enthusiastically. "Is that okay with you, Michael?"

"Sure, I guess. I mean, I, uh, didn't bring any swim trunks or anything."

Jay laughed. "That's perfect. We don't allow *clothing* in our hot tub anyway."

Scott somehow found the wooden spoon in the soapy water and swatted Jay's arm playfully. "You be good."

"Yes, Mom," Jay said without a hint of remorse. Then leaned over my shoulder and whispered, his hot breath brushing my ear, "It's settled. Naked tub in ten. I'm gonna go get it hot for you."

The glass slipped from my grasp, and soapy water splattered everywhere.

Jay's laughter could be heard echoing off the walls until the thud of the sliding door blocked him out.

"Don't let his mouth scare you. He's harmless.

Besides, he's got a *great* mouth," Scott said affectionately.

I ignored the burning blush of my ears and focused on fishing the glass out of the bubbles.

WAS IT WEIRD TO GO *UPSTAIRS* FOR AN OUTDOOR hot tub?

I wasn't sure, but, like a lost puppy, I followed Scott anyway.

We wove our way through a hallway and entered a large bedroom that spanned half the upstairs floor space. Their king-sized bed held court against the far wall, and was cloaked in a fluffy comforter embroidered with a bright floral pattern. Another huge television hung on the wall opposite the bed. Dressers consumed one side, while the other side contained a small sitting area, complete with two chairs and a love seat. Double French doors between the dressers led to their bathroom. I couldn't see much, but a sea of marble gleamed as I strained to check it out.

We exited through a sliding door next to the love seat. The smell of freshly cut grass slapped my nose as we walked out onto the upper deck, where the hot tub gurgled happily. Scott disappeared back into the house to grab towels.

I really didn't connect the dots of the hot tub sitting only a few feet from the entrance to their bedroom. Bookmark that for later. You'll want to reference this moment of gullible idiocy.

As I stared into the frothy water, I couldn't stop thinking about Jay's steamy breath on my neck. The tiny hairs prickled as my fingers tried to scratch the sensation away. I sucked in a deep breath, but an odd mix of terror, anticipation, and something I couldn't identify kept my heart racing—horniness, yeah, that was the other thing. Little Michael made *that* clear. The mixture of those emotions was a cocktail made for, well, a cock—and mine was ready to leap out of my shorts and be seen by the world. I was afraid it might break out into song like in a Disney movie.

Hmm. I wonder what Uncle Walt would name *that* character?

Never mind.

Scott and Jay were inside doing whatever they did before getting naked in a hot tub. They'd left me out to wait, or get ready, or, I don't know, play with the dogs. Three luminous fluff balls had tailed us and now swirled in constant motion around my feet.

I peered over the railing and took in the perfectly manicured yard. Bursts of pink, purple, and blue bordered the green expanse. At the far end, a small wooden pergola sheltered two benches and a bubbling fountain. There wasn't a bloom or blade out of place, and the towering fence encircling the garden ensured total privacy. Even the upper deck had light-brown wicker screens to shield the hot tub from the neighbors' view. Somewhere, on another plane of existence, a Japanese Zen master was pleased by Jay's effort.

"Am I throwing you in fully clothed?"

I nearly jumped over the railing as Jay stepped up behind me.

When I turned, my eyes widened at his naked body only inches away—and we're not talking AOL inches either. I staggered back a step, and the banister pressed into my back. He grinned at my discomfort.

My eyes ignored the command to stay at eye level, wandering down his perfectly tanned and toned physique. His shoulders were even rounder than I remembered, and he had those tiny nipples you just wanted to tickle and call *my little buddy*.

That's not weird. That's what you call them, right? Anyway.

Before I could vomit—I mean, say anything—he stepped forward and gripped the bottom of my T-shirt with both hands.

"Arms up, mister," he commanded.

My arms *flew* skyward as if a dozen policemen had guns trained on me.

His grin widened as he slowly pulled my shirt

upward, revealing my abs. He teased my skin, dragging my shirt so the fabric barely tickled it on the way up. I couldn't stop a shiver.

"Stop that!" Scott's voice shattered the moment. I wanted to thank him for saving me, but couldn't find my voice. "At least wait to strip him until I can watch."

Thanks a lot, Scott. Nice save, dude.

Off went my shirt. Jay looked down at my chest, shot me a devious grin, then tossed my shirt over the banister into the yard. I was so stunned that I forgot the guys and turned my head to watch the shirt flutter to the ground. The sensation of fingers around my happy trail, fumbling with my jeans button, spun my head back around. Jay was on his knees with my button between his fingers. Scott knelt behind him, his eyes glued to the show Uncle Walt never intended.

I didn't know what to do. *Shit*. These guys were a couple. Were they actually coming on to me? Could I get naked with *married* guys?

Technically, guys couldn't get married back then, but you know what I mean. Wait, maybe that technicality actually allowed me to do this? Maybe I was legally bound to get naked. Gay rights or equal marriage rights or something super important might depend on my nakedness. This was a patriotic duty!

In that moment, I decided to give myself to the cause.

I spread my arms out wide, placed my hands on the banister, and arched my back so my head was hovering over open yard. Jay had full access to do whatever he pleased to that little button.

No, the *actual* button. My other thing wasn't little. Really.

Stop laughing.

I heard Scott whisper, "Oh my god. Look at him."

They hadn't unbuttoned my jeans yet. Confused, I looked down to find Jay staring up at my eyes and Scott reaching a hand out to touch my abs. A second later, his fingertips brushed my skin and my whole body convulsed.

All three of us grinned.

Then Jay ripped my jeans off and tossed them over the railing into the yard.

8

———

SANDWICHES SATISFY

I was first to climb into the hot tub, anxious to get my pasty-white nakedness out of the open air. According to the temperature gauge I stubbed my toe on, the water was a steamy one hundred and four degrees. I sank below the froth and edged toward the safety of the far wall of the tub. When I looked up, Scott's balls were swinging at eye level as he descended the two steps and submerged himself. I was too startled to be embarrassed. They were low hangers and happy to see me.

Jay entered immediately after Scott. He was fully erect, so his balls were huddled tightly together. I swear one of them winked at me as I snuck a peek.

Can balls wink?

Anyway.

We each claimed a separate side of the watery

square. The boys remained pressed against their respective edges, their bodies simmering below the surface of the water, only their heads exposed to the evening air. I dipped down and doused my hair, then smeared it back with my hands as I re-emerged. The heat felt amazing.

"So, no boyfriend?" Jay asked as he wiped water from his face.

"I had one." My eyes dropped. "Guess it didn't work out."

Scott's voice was flush with empathy. "What happened? It's okay if you don't want to talk about it."

I gave him a weak smile that barely curled my lips. "His ex-wife threatened to cut him off from his kids. It was them or me. I can't really blame him. No father could walk away from his boys." My voice broke.

Scott waded to my wall. The hairs of his legs tickled mine as he sat beside me. "I'm sorry. That must've been hard. How old were the kids?"

"Five and three. Cade and Christian." My smile was genuine as I recalled their names.

Scott mirrored my expression. "When did all this happen? I mean, when did things end?"

"December, right before Christmas. That's, what, three, four months ago?"

Jay finally entered the conversation. "How long were you together?"

I snorted. "I knew you'd ask that. Just three months—but he was my first, and we were together pretty much every day of those three months. On the weekends he had the kids, I did everything with them. I think I fell in love with the kids as much as I did him."

"Three months may not seem like much, but it matters, especially if he was your first," Scott said, ever the caretaker. His arm rose out of the water and wrapped around my shoulders. I let myself melt in his embrace, needing to borrow from his strength. "If you ever want to talk about it, we're here. Okay?"

I looked up and met his eyes.

Given the earlier aggressive undressing and Jay's very happy penis, this wasn't how I expected our aquatic adventure to go, but it felt *right* somehow. I could see in Scott's eyes the care and concern of one who understood and wished he could relieve my pain. We'd known each other for, what, eight hours? Yet I felt his sincerity, his empathy.

Scott was one of the good ones.

Suddenly, Jay's leg pressed against my other side, and his arm wrapped around my shoulders on top of Scott's. Startled, I turned to see the same empathy in his eyes I'd seen from Scott. For some reason, that startled me. I had no reason to think Jay was any less of a good man, but the fact he demonstrated the same concern as his partner…I hadn't expected that either.

"There are a million bastards out there who just want something, mostly to get into your pants. You're a handsome guy, Michael. They'll be all over you. Whatever you do, don't lose the man who's still hurting because he misses those boys. He's the most amazing man I've met in a long time."

Scott and Jay looked across at each other and shared a smile. On cue, they both wrapped their other arms around me and formed a group hug. There was nothing sexual about it, only the warmth of two men responding to a third who didn't even know he needed the support.

God, I needed that hug.

Right there, in the middle of the hot tub, wrapped in the arms of two incredibly hot, naked dudes, the pent-up emotion from the loss of Carter and the boys poured out of me. The harder my shoulders heaved, the tighter they held me.

No one spoke.

Ten, maybe twenty minutes passed—long enough for the hot tub's auto-timer to shut off, forcing Jay to leave the circle to reset it.

Scott reached up and wiped the tears from my

cheeks. His fingers were gentle—and pruny. We'd been in the hot tub a while.

I took his hand and ran my finger over the elderly ridges and smiled. "I think we've stayed in past the manufacturer's recommended guideline."

He snorted, clearly surprised by my quick return to humor.

Before he could reply, Jay appeared and splashed more water on us than was required by the two-foot journey. "Don't even think about getting out of this water, gentlemen."

I tried to make some smart-ass response, but Jay snatched my breath by plonking onto my lap, straddling my legs, and planting a deep kiss on my lips. When he pulled back, his eyes smoldered, while mine were Puss in Boots wide. He laughed and floated out of my lap.

"Well, that wasn't very fair, Jay. Why'd you get him first?" Scott asked.

My whole head snapped toward him, terrified, as his mouth closed in and locked over my own. Where Jay had been passionate and aggressive, Scott's lips were soft and tender, his tongue teasing mine, tempting it, but going no further. When he pulled back, my whole body surged forward to follow, begging to stay connected.

He grinned as we parted, then turned to Jay and

winked. "Come over here, babe. You know I hate it when you're so far away."

So far away? He was in the same hot tub. What the hell?

Before Bambi could run for the woods, *two* sets of lips, *two* tongues, dove forward in a mingling of barbecue and heat that sent my head spinning. I tried to resist, to pull back, but I was squished against the tub's wall. There was nowhere to go. Somewhere in the back of my mind, the tiny angel who so often seared me with her acidic guilt was screaming, but everything in me wanted them, wanted *both* of them. I felt myself sink into the steaming water and surrender to their desire.

Scott pulled back, and Jay resumed his straddle position. His lips, no longer tentative, attacked, and I responded in kind. Our mouths were a blur, and I moaned as shivers shot across my skin.

Then Scott took over. My eyes were closed, but I knew the difference in their touch and taste now, the intimate subtlety of Scott's lips grazing my neck, his fingers tracing my chest under the water. He gripped around my waist and lifted me up, his lips never slow-ing. Fire bloomed as Jay pressed firmly against me, the evidence of his desire grinding, parting my cheeks with strong hands. My head fell back and both men's mouths descended, teeth teasing my skin, tongues tasting my sweat.

And then the timer sounded and the hot tub shut off again.

Jay reached for the dial to reset our time, but Scott stayed his hand. "Let's move inside."

Scott grabbed my hand and led me out of the tub. I reached for a towel and he playfully slapped my hand away. He took the cloth and, with deliberate slowness, found every drop of water on my body and dabbed it dry. Jay kept ruining his effort as he slid his dripping torso against me from behind, nibbling my neck and ears.

Amused, Scott handed him a towel. "Since you keep getting him wet, you do his back."

Jay smirked. "Oh, I plan to."

I leaned into his touch.

Then it was Jay's turn to take my hand. He led me back inside and closed the sliding door, then guided me to the bed where Scott lay waiting with the covers turned back.

I looked from Scott to Jay, checking for signs that either might be uncomfortable inviting a third man into their bed, but all I saw was acceptance and desire. Scott quieted the last of my worry as his hand reached out and pulled me down next to him on the pillow-like comforter. We scooted to the head of the bed where the pillows lay. Jay joined us, stretching his six-foot frame beside me.

We stared in silence for a long moment, then each of them bent their heads to attack a nipple. I nearly peed the bed right there. Scott and Jay broke into a fit of laughter at the horror written across my face.

"I might need to pee."

Jay snorted. Scott came up for air and pointed. "Go on. It's through that door."

Now a tad self-conscious, I padded into the Taj Mahal of bathrooms. Seriously. This thing was insane, and probably spanned the whole length of my apartment. There were three sinks spread along a long vanity wall, each with its own mirror held in modern black frames. The sinks themselves were clear glass bowls that sat atop the counter.

Who needs three sinks? I thought, since there were only two of them.

Three marble steps led up to a tub that looked like it could seat six people. It had jets like those in the hot tub outside. I definitely had tub envy.

Then I saw the shower. Holy sprinklers, Batman.

It was basically a glass box with shower heads sticking out of *everywhere*. It looked more like a car wash than a shower, and I wondered if giant roller things with rags attached would descend from the ceiling if I turned it on. There was a weird silver wand-like attachment hanging on the wall I didn't recognize. I guessed it was used for giving the dogs a bath, but made a mental note to ask later.

Satisfied with my tour of the palatial potty, I used the actual potty, thankful for the moment to process everything that had happened—was *about* to happen. I was pretty sure there were two men outside the door expecting a second half to this ballgame. Hell, I might've wanted it more than they did, and I wasn't even sure what game we were playing. I took a few deep breaths, shook the tinkle off my dinkle, then dabbed it with toilet paper for good measure. I didn't want them to think I was a drippy barbarian.

As I passed the sinks, I spotted a decanter filled with mouthwash and rinsed the barbecue away. I chuckled, thinking how they'd make me taste it again soon.

The image staring back in the mirror grabbed my eye as I set the decanter down. I stood straight and stuck my chest out. *Huh.* I looked *good*. The skinny kid who would never take his shirt off at the beach actually had muscles and definition. I had *abs*. I grinned, almost giddy. Was this what it felt like to be proud of how you looked? I'd never known that before.

"Can we get in on some of that? Or are you going

to hoard all the goods?" Jay's voice snapped me out of my Miss America crowning moment.

It was my turn to make them jump.

I turned and ran back into the bedroom and leapt on top of them. Scott tried to roll out of the way, but I grabbed his shoulders and pulled him into the pile. In a blink, three grown men were wrestling and tickling and laughing like kids at a slumber party.

Okay, naked kids who had just made out and were about to do worse—not any slumber party I remembered, but it was definitely going to be fun.

Scott freed himself and trotted into the bathroom. "Now look what you've done. *I* have to pee!" He stuck his tongue out and laughed.

"I'm gonna make you use that tongue, mister," I called without thinking, then clamped my hands over my mouth as I realized how forward I'd sounded.

Jay was sitting up on his knees, his sculpted chest and impressive manhood facing me. He saw my innocence, the way I struggled with sexuality. His head cocked, and I swear something in his eyes clicked. He leaned his long body over mind, then slowly pressed his weight against me, while holding his head up. His eyes never wavered. When our mouths were inches apart, he whispered, "You know you're safe with us, right?"

My throat caught. Safe? In the laundry list of

emotions and fears, *safety* hadn't ever come to mind. What was he implying? Would other men physically hurt me? Or did he mean they were a safe place to talk and share? He hadn't been the nurturing one of the pair, and I didn't know quite how to take his declaration.

It must've shown because he rolled over onto one elbow and spoke softly. "We've been together a long time, and we rarely do this sort of thing. Actually, I think you're the third guy we've ever done this with— in eight years. I love Scott more than life itself, and I know he loves me the same way, but we both have this need…" He stopped and his eyes drifted as he thought. "It's hard to explain. We want—no, we *need* —to share our love with someone. We are enough, the two of us, but we know we want more. Am I making any sense?"

I really didn't know what he meant—any of it— except for the part about how they loved each other. Ray Charles could've seen that. The rest? Not so much.

Scott returned and blanketed my other side with his body. "Don't let him get all sappy." Scott gave Jay a smart-ass grin. "That's *my* job in this house and no one gets to take it from me."

My heart pulled at his words. I couldn't explain it, but I really liked these guys, each of them, both of them, together and separately. How was that even possible?

I chuckled. "Yes, sir. You're the sappy one. Got it."

He gave me a gentle peck on the cheek. "What Jay means is that you have nothing to fear in this house. We'd love you to stay, to get to know you more, but we also get this is new to you and is probably overwhelming. Don't feel you have to keep going if you're not comfortable."

"How did you—"

"Oh, Michael, we could spot a newborn gay a mile away." Scott grinned.

"Enough mush." Jay shoved him off me with a laugh and pressed himself down, chest to chest once again. This time he didn't hold himself up. His mouth pressed back into mine as his hands roamed freely, kneading my arms and sides until they reached my butt. He moaned, and I felt his erection return, growing against my own. The friction of our dicks pumping and stretching sent lightning up my spine.

We passed each other back and forth, me to Scott, then to Jay, then the two of them together. I watched as they kissed with the familiarity of time and experience, the depth of love that only comes to those who've lived a lifetime together. It warmed my heart to see their passion for each other, and made me long for the same.

They turned their attention back to me. Scott leaned over, kissing me, stroking my now-throbbing penis, and whispered, "I want you inside me."

Then Jay whispered from behind, "And I want to be deep inside you."

My head spun back and forth. I didn't know where to look or who to listen to. What was I supposed to do?

Waves of exhilaration battered my senses at the idea of having *both* of them—*at the same time*. I'd never thought of such a thing.

Scott rolled over onto his side, urging me to spoon him from behind. I heard the pop of a bottle cap and squirt of liquid, then felt Jay's slick hand wrap around my shaft, teasing the skin with moisture and soaking my head with slippery pleasure. His hand turned toward Scott and he fingered his hole, earning a squirm and moan. Jay leaned back and squirted more lube on his palm, but I was captivated by Scott's hand reaching behind and gripping me. He pulled me into him, pressing back, nudging himself closer and me in deeper. I spasmed with ecstasy as the last of my length entered his body and his head craned back to kiss me.

Then Jay's freshly saturated hand found my hole and I grunted in Scott's ear, pushing hard at the surprise of Jay's touch. I felt him clinch around me and stars flashed. Then Jay pressed inside me and I thought my heart would burst out of my chest. He pushed, I pressed back, Scott arched to drive me deeper. We were clumsy at first, but quickly learned to time our thrusts. Again and again, the three of us became one.

Jay kissed my neck while Scott's tongue drove into my mouth. I reached around Scott and grabbed his throbbing uncut cock and began stroking, teasing his head, toying with the fold of skin now stretched taut. Then I slid my palm down, squeezing tighter. His mouth released mine, and Jay leaned in, stealing my mouth away, kissing me deeply.

The pressing became pumping, then grinding and thrusting. I could feel Scott quicken in his shortened breaths and the pulsing of his cock, so I stroked it faster, alternating between firm and teasingly loose. His hole responded, caressing my cock with a throbbing constriction, a sudden clutch that made me cry out. Scott's body shivered and convulsed as his cum exploded across my hand and his body. Surge after surge coated him, and I could smell the salty sex smeared across his skin. He reached back and held me, telling me not to stop, to drive onward, begging for more.

Jay growled in my ear and his gentleness

vanished. He slammed himself inside me as hard and deep as he could, before pulling back and ramming into me again. Something snapped at his renewed vigor and I drove myself further into Scott. He cried out, "God, yes, don't stop!"

I didn't.

I couldn't.

Jay clutched my chest with both hands and he pumped me so fast I could barely keep up—Jay into me…me into Scott…Jay…Scott…

Sweat poured down my forehead. My mind and vision were blurred. I couldn't think, only felt the wild, unhindered passion flowing through the three of us.

Jay's body tensed, his cock throbbed, and I knew he was close. The thought of him inside me pushed my already addled mind over the edge, and I lost control, spilling myself into Scott again and again. I whispered "I'm sorry" in his ear, but his grip on my hips tightened, drawing me into him, refusing my pleas.

Then Jay shouted, "Oh god, I'm coming!"

He slammed again and again until I felt him empty inside me. All three of us shivered, and Jay's arms reached beyond my shoulders to pull Scott close, sandwiching me in between. I kissed Scott's neck as Jay, tenderly, did the same to mine.

We dared not move.

Our breathing slowed.

Our pulses eased.

***

SOMETIME IN THE MIDDLE OF THE NIGHT, I WOKE UP. My sleep had been peaceful, dreamless, something I hadn't enjoyed in a while. Nature had removed me from Scott and ejected Jay from me, but our arms were still tangled and our bodies mingled tightly.

I lifted Jay's arm and laid it against his side, careful to not wake either of them, then looked down at Scott. I reached out and moved a stray strand of hair from his forehead as I watched the rise and fall of his chest. Then I turned and studied Jay. They were so different, yet so similar. Jay's dark features made my blood boil, while Scott's tender heart made my own skip a beat. They were each beautiful and passionate in their own ways.

I honestly couldn't decide which I liked better.

Is that weird? Isn't one supposed to captivate more than the other? Aren't we made to be with *one* other person who blinds us to all others?

That's what I'd been taught, at least about straight relationships. I'd just assumed gay ones worked the same.

Scott and Jay made me challenge those lessons, challenge what might—

Scott's fingers grazed my chest, and I turned to face his opened eyes. He smiled. With his disheveled hair and genuine grin, my heart melted. I leaned down and kissed him. Before I knew what was happening, he'd gripped me back into stiffness and slid me inside him again. This time he begged me to take him slowly, to press and pull and savor every motion. My skin pimpled with excitement as I slid in and out. I could feel his body react to each thrust.

For a fleeting moment, I worried Jay might wake and be jealous, but that idea shattered when I felt his lips against my neck again. Then his hands gripped my abs. He kissed me like that for a while, letting Scott and me have our moment, then slid himself back into my still-moist hole.

When we fell asleep after our second time, nature didn't remove either of us from the other.

We woke as one.

9

COFFEE TALK

"Wait, you slept with a *couple*?" Jason leaned across the table, eager and incredulous.

I nodded. "Yeah. We kind of did it twice. I mean, after dinner and the hot tub."

"You actually had a *date* with a couple? Are you serious?" Dwayne perked up.

"I don't know that I'd call it a date. We met online, then ran into each other randomly at softball. They invited me over for dinner. I was dessert."

Dwayne and Jason shared a look as Katie ambled over. "I've never seen the two of you looks so out of sorts. This must be good. Spill it."

She refilled our coffee mugs as Jason blurted, "Boy Scout over there banged a couple last night."

"What?" She spilled Dwayne's pour all over the table.

"Technically, I only banged one of them. The other one—"

"Enough!" She held up the palm not laden with coffee. "I don't need details. I get the squishy picture."

As she walked away, I grinned and winked at Jason. "It was pretty squishy."

Dwayne threw the napkin he'd been using to clean up the coffee at me, then pointed a finger at Jason. "*You,* stop encouraging him. I'm trying to raise a respectable gay here."

"Don't look at me, grandpa. I'm actually impressed. The boy scored more last night than I have all year."

"*Not helping!*" Dwayne tossed another soaked napkin on his plate and got to his feet. "I'm getting more napkins. You two behave."

Jason and I laughed as he headed to the counter. During my post-Carter period, Jason and I had become friends. I'd always liked him, but more as one of his lovesick followers than as a real person. Now that those emotions were thankfully out of my system, I'd come to enjoy his sarcastic wit, especially when he aimed it at Dwayne. They'd been friends since the dawn of time, and I could see that closeness through their interactions. Regardless of who was speaking, there was usually an undertone of caring and love, overlaid with sass and fire. They were a perfect odd couple, and now Jason joined most of our lunch dates.

"Are you going to see them again?" He was like a little kid. I'd never seen him so excited.

"I guess so. They both play softball in the league, so I'll definitely see them there."

"No, dummy, *see* them again—as in *get naked* again?"

"Uh, I don't know. We didn't talk about it." I was suddenly uncomfortably aware of Dwayne's shadow darkening the table.

"I think you should. Sounds like they might be open to a throuple."

Dwayne plopped down dramatically beside Jason and elbowed him to scoot over. "Don't listen to his nonsense. Come to think of it, *never* listen to Jason again unless he's singing—and then, don't pay attention to his words, just the music."

Jason laughed. "Let the boy be happy, old man. Times have changed since you invented the wheel. Throuples are hot."

"You can't even get a *couple* to work. What would you know?"

"You wound me, good sir." Jason mimicked a bow from his seat.

"You two are better than television," I said. "I don't know if they're looking for a third or a throuple or whatever. They said they don't even do three-ways that often, that I was the first in a few years. We may never see each other naked again."

"Why do I hear disappointment in your voice when you say that?" Jason needled.

I hesitated. *Was* there disappointment in my voice? *Did* I want to get naked with them again? If so, was all this purely physical? I'd never heard of a throuple, much less considered one. The very idea went against monogamy and every other principle my preacher dad ever taught me. Hell, getting naked with them had shattered most of those principles. "I…I don't know."

Dwayne leaned over and put his hand on my arm. "You had fun. That's good. Don't read more into it than it was—just sex."

I looked up, unsure I agreed.

"I know losing Carter and the kids was hard, but jumping into something like this is…well, it's not the right thing for you. Just trust me. Your heart is exposed and raw right now."

"Sounds like his ass is raw too." Jason barked a laugh, and Dwayne involuntarily spit coffee on me.

"Hey!"

"Sorry, kiddo," Dwayne said through gasps. "Jason won that round."

10

SOFTBALLS AND YOUNG BALLS

Three uneventful weeks passed.

Jason played a couple more gigs and Dwayne met a new kid—I mean, guy. This one was a twenty-three-year-old who'd just moved from Florida, or Atlanta, I wasn't paying much attention. He babbled about the child's smile and eyes for an hour, only allowing Jason to interrupt a few times. It was good to see him beaming, even if the object of his affection was out of reach.

We'd talked a few times about his attraction to guys half his age, and about the odds anything would actually work out with them, but Dwayne played it off as though he didn't want anything serious. He reasoned, if nothing came of it other than some flirtation or sex, he was fine with that.

I never bought that. Despite his perpetually positive attitude and smile, I could feel the loneliness in him. I could see it in his eyes when he'd talk about someone from his past, or when one of his younglings wouldn't work out.

At least, for now, he was happy and hopeful.

I left the diner and headed to softball practice. My new team had practiced once each week since the tryouts. We were terrible, but it was fun to learn a new sport.

Our coach met me in the parking lot before my first practice. She was a short, stocky woman in her midthirties and looked like she could drop me to the ground before I could cry for help. I liked—and feared—her the moment we met. Before we walked away from my car, she looked at my closed trunk and asked if I needed help with my equipment. I held up a glove and shook my head, laughing. She seemed perturbed. I later learned that serious players owned their own bats and carried them in fancy bags with their jersey number embroidered on the side. The lack of such accoutrement told her all she needed to know about my experience level.

Sergeant Coachie took her softball seriously.

I was introduced as the new superstar pitcher. Clearly, no one had told Coachie I'd never played the position before, and I didn't bother to correct her. She and I spent much of the practice getting me used to hitting a tiny spot behind the plate. It was a repetitive motion that came naturally, and I quickly learned to control the ball's movement with various spins.

Who knew? Maybe I was a slow-pitch stud.

I didn't see Scott and Jay. They were both B-level players and their team didn't practice on the same day as mine. I thought we'd see more of each other when the season started, but I later learned that B-level games were usually scheduled at different times from C. That sucked, but I figured we could find other ways to meet up. Sure, I was hungry for more hot-tub time, but something inside me was also intrigued—and terrified—by the idea of dating a couple. What would that be like? Could it even work? I had so many questions.

There was part of me still wary of natural jealousies and the perception of others, along with a hundred other fears plaguing my PK mind. A throuple wasn't something sanctioned in the Good Book, and it certainly wouldn't be approved of by the wolf pack. That might even send my dad over the edge, and I didn't want to endanger the tenuous truce we'd established.

It all sucked. I really liked the guys, both of them. I'd talked to a number of guys online about the idea, and every one of them said jealousy usually killed throuples. The third would fall for one or the other, or one of the original couple would fall out with the third. There were far more reasons for a throuple not to work than for it to live happily ever after.

On top of everything, I still struggled with the basics of making a relationship work. The only one I'd ever known went from zero to sixty in one night, then crashed and burned worse than the Death Star. If I couldn't handle dating one man, what made me think I could succeed with two egos and personalities, and everything else that came with dating an already established pair?

In the end, I never pursued another dinner or date or *whatever* that was. I ran into the guys a few times, when our games were scheduled close together, and they were always friendly, but I never chased that dream.

I guess the little angel had found her voice again— or a strong pair of handcuffs.

Wait, that should be the little devil with the hand-cuffs, shouldn't it?

11

ZOO GUY

The next couple of months passed in a blur. Basketball season kicked into high gear, and I officiated either high school or small college games five or six nights a week. Between work during the day, squeezing in gym time to avoid my roommate's evil eye, and refereeing, there wasn't much time left for anything else.

That worked out just fine. It kept my mind off how much I missed Carter and the boys.

Midway through February, high schools entered playoffs season. They'd start with Districts, then Regionals, and eventually, the big kahuna—the State Championship. Every high school player in the state wanted to make it to their version of The Dance. What might surprise most folks is how much every referee in the state also wanted to make it to the elite end of the playoffs. There were only three officials in the finals of the State Championship, and we all wanted to be one of those highly talented officials.

Unfortunately, there were politics in the world of officiating, and, while I was a skilled referee, I wasn't great at *that* game. The result was an earlier end to my season than I'd hoped, just like those high schoolers whose teams missed a shot at the buzzer.

Oh well.

Send in Dwayne, coach. He'll save the day!

THE FIRST FRIDAY IN MARCH MARKED THE BEGINNING of the State Championship. You know, the one I wasn't invited to be part of? I wasn't bitter. Really.

Dwayne proposed we go to the Chute. He was a regular there, but I'd never been. Were gay bars all different? Were the gays who went to one bar different from those at another? I had so many questions. Dwayne rolled his eyes and laughed. His only answer was, "Come with me and see for yourself."

So I did.

The Chute sat at the end of a short strip mall. It didn't look like much from the street, but it sprawled almost the whole length and depth of the mall building. While the other businesses won street-facing space, the Chute won the battle for actual floor space.

We got there around ten, well before the gay witching hour when most of the boys would show up. What was it with gay men and their nocturnal internal clocks? Were they born with it? Was it somehow instilled in them at a certain age?

Did I just make the *nature versus nurture* argument over time and bar attendance? Wow. I needed a drink.

But it was like magic. At eleven thirty, the bars would be empty. At midnight—on the dot—they'd bulge at the seams.

The bars, not the boys. Although, now that I think about it, you're right—some of the boys bulged nicely too.

Stop distracting me.

We walked past the doorman, who nodded to me, then stood and hugged Dwayne and called him "Sugar" in greeting. That would *definitely* come back to haunt him. I loved nicknames.

The bar was exactly as he'd described. The front opened onto a large dance floor surrounded by carpeted boxes for sitting and watching. One lonely guy swayed to pounding bass beneath the swirling lights of lasers and strobes. At one end of the dance floor were stairs leading to the DJ booth, and at the other end was the bar, which was actually pretty cool. A tall case holding liquor of every color and variety towered in the center. Around it, the bar top formed a rectangle wide and long enough to house three or four bartenders at any one time. At that moment, Dwayne and I had the place to ourselves—except for the dancer and one bartender, who waved as we approached.

"Back so soon?" he asked as he leaned over the bar to hug Dwayne.

"Is it Friday?" Dwayne grinned. "Donny, meet Michael, the Luke to my Yoda."

I quirked a brow at Dwayne, then turned and offered Donny my hand to shake. He looked at me funny, then snuck a glance at Dwayne.

Dwayne smirked. Donny shrugged. I didn't get it.

He shook my hand, a firm, manly shake that held on a little longer than was necessary. His gray eyes were warm and locked onto mine without flinching.

Dwayne got his usual bucket of limes with a splash of liquid, and I sipped my Coke, earning another odd grin from Donny.

He sure grinned a lot.

A few sips later, Dwayne dragged me away from the bar to inspect the back, which opened into a show bar similar to the one I'd experienced at the Connection. It could hold a couple hundred patrons facing a wide stage with giant curtains and glaring spotlights. Small tables for three or four filled the middle of the room, allowing open space around the stage and in the back, where the bars held court. Another lonely bartender was setting up his station. He looked up, waved, and yelled Dwayne's name, like he was Norm in *Cheers*, then resumed his work.

We wandered back to the main bar and grabbed stools directly in front of Donny. He was busy hauling bottles, filling ice bins, and placing clean glasses on their easy-to-reach shelves below the bar. As we sat, I caught him glance up, then look down quickly. Sandy blond curls flopped as his head darted below the bar.

He was tall, six two or three I guessed, so being sneaky with his peeky wasn't easy.

Now I was curious about Mr. Sneaky Peeky.

Dwayne and I talked about our uneventful weeks while Donny worked. I watched him out the corner of my eye, trying to be casual. I clearly wasn't.

Dwayne looked up as Donny passed, a heavy crate of wine bottles making his bare arms bulge. "Michael thinks you're cute. You two should talk."

Donny stopped in front of us and looked from Dwayne to me.

"What? Wait. I didn't say anything. Where'd that —" I stammered. Dwayne and Donny giggled like schoolgirls.

Dwayne said he had to pee and disappeared.

Donny resumed his box-hauling, so for the first time that night I got a good look. His hair curled slightly at the ends and was cut short except for some floppy coils that bounced around his forehead. It was neat but messy at the same time. I wanted to reach up and push them back every time he talked. As he passed one of the other bartenders, I realized he was taller than I'd thought before, probably six four. Most guys that tall had trouble gaining muscle. Donny clearly didn't. His arms were ripped, and the white Fruit of the Loom tank top he wore was straining across his chest. He was sweating from his work, and the fabric revealed more than it covered. I watched with admiration as his headlights panned the room on high beam. He wasn't weightlifter huge—you know, that neck-bigger-than-his-head look—but he was nicely muscled.

I'd say he was handsome, but not strikingly so. He wouldn't turn every head in the bar when he walked in, but his personality and infectious smile pushed him from a seven to a solid eight.

I've always been a sucker for a nice smile. Color me romantic.

I was so wrapped up in cataloging his looks that I missed the part where he stopped working and turned.

Oh shit.

"Need something?" he asked with that frustrat-ingly cute grin, then threw his head back to toss a curl out of his eyes.

I woke up. "Uh, no. I'm good. Thanks."

His grin broadened. He extended his hand across the bar. "My name's Donny McLeren."

We'd already shaken hands, but it would be rude to leave him hanging, so I took his palm again, careful to mirror his firm grip from before. "I'm Michael Reed. Nice to meet you."

His grip was solid again, warm. He felt good. An involuntary shiver ran up my arm.

He released my hand and gave me a shallow head dip like you'd see in old movies about medieval England. "It's my pleasure, Mr. Reed."

"So, you work here all the time?"

What a stupid question. I mentally slapped my forehead.

He nodded. "Most weekends. I work at the zoo during the week though."

"The zoo?" My eyes widened. "What do you do there? I've never been to the Nashville Zoo."

He ran a hand through his hair, a gesture that made his bicep flex and my heart beat a little quicker.

"I'm the cat guy."

Huh. My head tilted. "The cat guy?"

"I know what you're thinking. Not *those* cats.

Think tigers and lions. They're cats too, and I'm their keeper."

"That's *so* cool," slipped out before I got my Coke to my lips. What was I, eight? Gah!

"You should come by sometime. I'll show you around. Nashville actually has a great zoo."

Dwayne walked up. "Zoo? What did I miss? Are you threatening to throw him to the lions?" He laughed at his own joke, not realizing that's *exactly* what we'd been talking about.

"You should come too, old man. You'd like it," Donny teased.

Dwayne shook his head and downed the last of his drink. "Nope. No zoo for me. You two young bucks enjoy that."

The trickle of guys whose internal clocks needed adjusting streamed in, so we said our goodbyes and headed to the door. Dwayne wanted to get home before it got too late, and I was tired from reffing all week.

As I pushed the glass door open, I felt a groping in my back pocket and practically leapt out of my jeans. I spun to find the doorman pulling his fingers out. He winked at me and wiggled the offending fingers in a tiny gay wave. I was so stunned that I'd walked all the way to Betty before checking inside the pocket he'd violated.

There, scrawled on a bar napkin, was Donny's name and number. I guess he thought I needed a reference point, because he left two words below his number:

Zoo Guy.

12

HORSES ARE FOR HEALING

Katie gave me a peck on the head as she set my pancakes down with a flourish. "You look good today, baby." She winked at Dwayne and skipped merrily back to the kitchen.

Maybe the *Cheers* folks were on to something. It *is* pretty cool to go where everybody knows your name.

"You and Donny seemed to hit it off last night."

"I guess. He seems nice." I shrugged. "The zoo thing is pretty cool."

Dwayne pointed his fork at me. "Listen here, mister, you need to pull your head out of your ass and get back on the horse—or under it, if that's your thing." He grinned, proud of his gay dad joke.

I rolled my eyes. "Yeah, I know. I've just been really busy with basketball lately."

"Oh no you don't. You were pissy all last week because you didn't get past Regionals. Your season is over. There's nothing taking up your precious time now. Call Donny. Go see lions or tigers or whatever he keeps. At least, see *his* tiger. Lord knows, Katie and I would love for you to get laid. I love ya, but you've been a lousy lunch partner lately."

"Aren't you the same gay sherpa who was scolding me for sleeping with a couple not that long ago?"

"That was different. You were being a mindless slut for your own empty pleasure." He snorted. "This is about *my* happiness and welfare. I'm perfectly happy to whore you out if it'll put you in a better mood. It'll certainly make these lunches more enjoyable."

"Sorry," I mumbled.

His voice softened. "I'm not complaining. Carter was your first, and I know how much you fell in love with his boys. I just want you to be happy again."

"Here, here," Katie chirped from behind me. The silky scent of brewed Kona beans wafted by as she leaned across the table. "Honey, you call that cat man. He sounds like just what you need right now."

"Cat man? Is he a superhero now?" I quipped.

"Only if he wears a tight leather outfit." She smirked, then put one hand on her hip in that *I'm a teapot* pose. "If he can make you smile again, he'll be a superhero in my book."

As she drifted to her next table, I looked up to find Dwayne chuckling. "She's not wrong, ya know?"

"Alright. Fine. I'll call him later. The napkin with his number is on my nightstand."

"Already keeping him near your bed. I love it."

I couldn't help but laugh. Dwayne could always get me.

AROUND TWO O'CLOCK, I WALKED INTO MY apartment to find Peter's things strewn about in neat piles. He'd arranged his clothes first by type, then by color. I grinned at his new sense of organization. He'd never cared before. Maybe the SEALs would be good for him.

I tiptoed my way through the minefield of tank tops and T-shirts until reaching my room, where the neat laundered stacks transformed into my unkempt piles of dirty clothes. The SEALs would never help me. It might take the whole navy to change my cluttered ways.

Donny's wadded napkin rested between a stack of quarters and a roll of toilet paper on my nightstand.

Don't be gross. The toilet paper was for nose blowing. I was too cheap to buy tissues.

I grabbed the napkin and headed back into the den. With seven spins of the rotary dial, Donny's warm bass echoed through the line. "Hello?"

"Uh, hey, Donny?"

"Michael." I could *hear* his smile. "It's nice to hear your voice again."

Now I was smiling. "It's nice to be heard. Um, I mean, it's nice to talk to you too."

He chuckled at my awkwardness.

"So," I blundered. "I was wondering if you might like to grab dinner or something sometime."

"That sounds great. I have to work tonight at seven, but could grab a quick bite before."

So soon? I didn't really know this guy, and was only doing this because Dwayne and Katie had guilted me into it, but my heart still skipped a beat. Why was I suddenly sweating?

"Awesome," was all I could get out.

We chatted a few more minutes, comparing areas of town, driving distances, and where might be a good, cheap spot in the middle. We were both on tight budgets. I liked that.

As I replaced the receiver, I couldn't help but feel a bubble of giddiness grow inside my chest. It had been months since I'd felt anything there—well, other than that murderous, stabbing sensation from the Carter breakup—but that doesn't count.

Maybe Dwayne was right. I just needed a good cowboy…I mean, horse…I mean, date. Yeah, *date*.

13

BARFLY

onny and I met at a ramshackle rotisserie chicken place around the corner from the Chute. It looked a lot like the diner, but with stained wood and the permanent smell of roasted chicken rather than coffee and bacon. They served tasty, healthy chicken, and the best vegetables in town. I loved their creamed corn, okra, and baked sweet potato slathered in cinnamon butter.

I'm not sure what I expected, having never been on a date with a bartender. The stereotype racing through my mind was of a guy whose pockets were perpetually overflowing with the phone numbers of patrons trying to get into his alcohol-stained pants.

Donny was *nothing* like my mental image.

Our conversation started with him asking if I'd read the latest book by…I don't remember. I've never cared for books. Movies always have more action and sound—and don't involve hours of reading. Donny, on the other hand, was a voracious reader. He enjoyed a good *Lord of the Rings* fantasy, which I respected, because those books would make a great movie one day. But he also enjoyed literary classics. He boggled my mind rattling off his reading list, a Santa's register of books he wanted to read but were patiently waiting in line for the one ahead to be completed first. Most were by British or French authors, with a few Russians added for their sexy accent.

I had a magazine on my nightstand. Did that count?

To escape the cultural hole I'd dug for myself by asking about his favorites, I changed the subject. "So, where are you from? Any brothers and sisters?"

He took a sip of tea. "I grew up in Ohio on a farm. My folks still live there, but they hired someone to run the place a few years ago. They're in their seventies now and putter around the house most days. My brother owns the place next door and practically lives on a tractor."

"You didn't want to work on the family farm?"

He laughed and held up his hands like I'd threatened to shoot. "Lord no. I grew up hauling hay, mucking stables, feeding pigs, and milking cows— and most of that had to be done before the sun came up every day. That's a lot more work than I'm willing to do every day."

My eyes roamed his bulky frame and grinned. "Looks like it did you *some* good."

He flexed a bicep in his best Arnold pose and flashed his pearly whites. "Hard work does build a body, true enough."

I wanted to pull my short sleeves down to cover my guns that now felt more like pea-shooters, despite their recent progress at the hands of Herr Peter.

"It was a great place to grow up." He got a faraway look in his eyes. "The farm's where I learned to love working with animals. We had everything you'd expect: cows, horses, chickens, pigs, you name it. The nearest vet was fifty miles away, so the whole family had to learn to take care of minor wounds or illnesses. I'd delivered babies by the time I was fourteen years old." I waited as he returned to the present. "The best part about working at the zoo is I don't have to wonder when we're going to slaughter an animal I've come to care about."

My face must've fallen because he nodded and continued. "Yeah, every year, especially the cows and pigs. There were a few we'd keep for breeding or milk, but a good number would go to the slaughterhouse. Aside from the grains we grew, that's how the farm paid the bills."

Our food came and I had a whole new respect for the chicken sitting before me.

Donny noticed me staring and made a peeping sound, then said in a squeaky voice, *"I can't believe you're going to eat me, you bad, bad man."*

He was grinning from ear to ear when I looked up, and we both broke into a fit of laughter. I turned eight shades of red, which only encouraged him. Before I knew it, tears were rolling down his cheeks and he was mimicking a sad chicken voice between guffaws.

The waitress appeared, looked back and forth between us, then bolted for the kitchen to get away from the crazy clucking gays. We shared a look and the tears flowed harder.

I couldn't remember the last time I'd laughed so hard my gut hurt.

As I finished the last of my actual chicken, the waitress braved another visit to our table, grabbed our empty plates, and tossed the bill down like it carried the plague. We both chuckled as we stood to walk to the register.

"Why don't you stop by the bar later?" Donny said. "It doesn't get busy until late, and there's only so much setup I can do. It'd be nice to have a little company."

I didn't know what to say. Would visiting him at his work be considered a second date? Was that even allowed? I'd have to check the Gay Handbook when I got home.

Screw the handbook. "Sure. Dwayne and I are supposed to touch base later. Mind if he tags along?"

"I love to see that old coot anytime. He's one of my favorites."

Old coot. That made me chuckle all the way to the car.

I WALKED INTO THE CHUTE AROUND NINE O'CLOCK to find Dwayne comfortably perched by the bar, Jack and Coke in hand, a tall glass stuffed full of lime wedges beside him on the counter. Donny was leaned over the bar toward him, and I thought the pair looked a little too conspiratorial. I stood just inside the doorway and watched for signs of an evil scheme. Dwayne was always up to something.

Donny's simple white tank from the night before had been replaced by a brown leather vest that hung open in the front. I was twenty yards away, but could see the definition of his furry pecs poking through. With the appearance of uncovered flesh, all fears of a conspiracy went out the window, and I made my way to the guys.

Dwayne raised his glass in greeting, his eyes twinkling with…something.

Oh boy.

Donny leaned over the bar to give me a quick hug. His vest popped fully open and my eyes widened as I lost count of the abs smiling up at me through their coating of neatly trimmed fur.

Holy mother of pearl, he was *ripped*. I hadn't seen that coming. I mean, I knew he was muscular, but not like *that*.

When he hugged me, the gay equivalent of a European kiss on either cheek, I squeezed to see if he was as firm as he looked. The muscles of his back were as hard as the bar's granite counter. I swooned a bit before letting go.

He must've noticed I'd held on longer than was specified in the Gay Handbook, because he and Dwayne shared a grin as I took a seat.

Donny excused himself to fetch another case of beer, giving Dwayne a chance to satiate his appetite for grilled Michael.

"So, how was dinner?" His voice carried the tone of someone who already knew the answer, but couldn't wait to hear how I'd respond. Yes, he was baiting me, and I knew it.

"It was good."

He waited. I shrugged. I could play too.

"Good? That's all I get? After all we've been through, that's it?"

"Forgive this one, sensei." I bowed my head formally, then looked up with a grin and rolled my eyes. "It was a nice dinner. Good food, pleasant conversation. That's about all there was."

He huffed. "Listen, *you*. You're *never* tight-lipped. That tells me as much as if you had diarrhea of the mouth, which is far more normal. Start talking before I use these limes on you right here in the middle of this bar." He grabbed the glass and pointed it threateningly.

We both laughed at the fruity gesture.

Is a fruity gesture normal in a gay bar?

Anyway.

I shook my head, then shrugged again. "I don't know what to say. He's a really nice guy. We met for rotisserie chicken, then went our separate ways because he had to work. I guess he liked me enough to invite me to the bar, so if stalking a bartender counts…"

"Let's not use *stalking* in a sentence, shall we? You have a history."

"Ha ha. Very funny. That was *one* time, and I was a virgin gay." I stuck my tongue out in the most mature gesture possible.

His brows shot up. "As I recall, there was a certain

nameless flight attendant who might disagree with that assessment. I don't believe he flew on *Virgin* Airlines."

Before I could respond, Donny appeared and set a glass of icy Coke in front of me. I raised it toward Dwayne, chuckled, and said, "Point to the old fart."

He tossed a lime at me.

"Wow. I step away for two minutes and you two are throwing garnish. What did I miss?" Donny leaned over with his elbows on the table and chin in his hands.

"*Nothing,*" I snapped, cutting off any smart-ass remark Dwayne might've had ready. "Dwayne was just being a snot."

"I was *educating* the boy on the meaning of the word *virgin*," Dwayne said, triumph in his eyes as he shot me a glare.

Dammit.

"Virgin? I take it we're not talking drinks, are we?" Donny quipped, suddenly appearing less confident about the quicksand on which he now stood.

"Ignore the senior citizen. Sometimes he forgets his name, where he is, all those things." I tried to laugh it off and change the subject. "So, tell us more about this zoo you work in. Sounds fun."

Donny cocked his head, thought a moment, then said, "Nope. Not gonna do it. If you want to know more, you'll have to come see it for yourself. I'll give you a guided tour."

Did he just ask me on *another* date? Holy virgin margarita. "That sounds awesome."

I glanced over to catch Dwayne's all-knowing smirk.

"You'll even get to meet some of the cats I hand-raised."

"Hand-raised?"

Donny nodded. "Sorry, I forget normal people don't know zoo-speak. Let me take care of this other guy. I'll explain in a minute. Be right back."

He darted to the opposite corner of the bar and began chatting with another customer. I'd almost forgotten he was working.

"Must've been some really good chicken. Do they serve *virgin* chicken there?" Dwayne's chirping woke me out of my daze. I'd been staring at Donny's ass…I mean jeans.

I snorted. "He's just being nice. Besides, the whole raising lions and tigers thing sounds totally cool."

"Totally cool? Since when does a Nashville boy turn valley?"

"It's, like, totally cool. Like, super cool, dude."

We giggled at our own goofiness before turning to watch Donny approach with a newly filled glass in each hand. "Can't let my boys go thirsty." His eyes locked onto mine as he smiled and set the glasses down. Tiny, adorable dimples I hadn't noticed before peeked from his cheeks.

We chatted for another half hour before the flood of gay-bar-loving patrons began streaming in. On cue, Dwayne and I synchro-drained the last of our drinks and set the glasses on the bar with a perfectly timed thud.

Even the Russian judge gave us a ten. Donny shook his head and laughed.

"Donny, it's been a pleasure, as always." Dwayne bowed in a most regal gesture.

The barkeep turned to me. "Three weeks from Sunday? The zoo is closed for cleaning and repairs. It'll just be you, me, and the staff. Oh, and Tina."

"Tina?"

He grinned. "Tina the tiny tiger. She's a Bengal weighing in at four hundred pounds, but she'll always be Tiny Tina to me. She was my first hand-raised cub. When I got her, she was the size of both of my palms put together. All fluff and massive golden eyes."

"So cool."

Dwayne speared me with an elbow.

Donny ignored him. "You should know, she's my character test. If she doesn't approve, we can't go out anymore—and she'll probably eat you."

I knew he was kidding, but he kept such a straight

face the color must've drained from my cheeks. He barked a laugh and waved the rag in his hand. "You kids drive safe. I hear there's gays out on the road at this hour."

Dwayne and I giggled our way out the door, turning more than a few of the new arrivals' heads. They were clearly curious about the guy who'd captured Donny's attention. I puffed out my chest, proud to be the guy someone else was jealous of for a change.

14

ZOOLANDER

Zoo day finally arrived.

I rose early and downed several cups of coffee before struggling to decide which pair of shorts went best with tiger fur. On my best days, I struggled with choosing clothes. How was I supposed to know what to wear when going on a date at a zoo? I gave in to ratty cargo shorts and a plain blue T-shirt.

Determined not to get lost, I carefully followed Zoo Guy's directions, which led me into a residential section in the heart of Nashville. I looked around, sure I'd made a wrong turn somewhere. Who would put a zoo in a neighborhood with, I don't know, *neighbors*? It seemed odd.

A moment later, a brightly colored wooden sign appeared. Apparently, the zoo *did* like neighbors after all.

I was surprised to find the parking lot nearly empty, then remembered Donny mentioned this was a staff-only day. My favorite bartender-slash-zookeeper was standing near the public entrance, a series of tall metal gates shaded by various trees to give patrons the feeling of entering a jungle. He waved as I nestled Betty into a front-row space a dozen yards away.

He wore jeans and a green shirt with 'Nashvegas' scrawled in white script on the chest.

Damn, he was tall. I'd somehow forgotten that.

"Hey!" He trotted over to the car as I climbed out, wrapping me in a quick hug before turning back to the gate.

I'd just arrived and already scored a hug. Sweet.

"Come on. I'll give you the tour before we go see my babies. You can help me feed the lions."

Oh shit. That sounded bloody dangerous. Like, *literally* bloody.

A thrill ran through me as I followed him onto the tan cobbles past the entrance. To either side, every six feet a wooden beam rose from the ground, supporting thick, rough-hewn rope that drooped between the posts. The sounds of a thousand birds chirping—and the smell of that same flock's poop—assaulted my senses. There wasn't a fence or cage to be seen.

"Aviary is first," Donny said, a few strides ahead of me.

I had guessed that on my own.

We turned to the right and walked into a wooden building with an insanely high ceiling. Netting made of the same thick rope I'd seen outside hung everywhere above. We stepped onto a wood-chipped path that wove through clumps of trees and bushes, giving the structure a natural, jungle-like feel. The peeping and squawking was overwhelming. Everywhere I looked, wings of every size and color flapped as their owners fluttered by. They seemed utterly disinterested in the humans strolling through their territory.

I'd been so distracted by the trees and birds that I'd lost Donny. I rounded two more bends in the path before nearly bumping into my gentle giant. He had a broad smile plastered across his face and a bird perched on each of his outstretched arms. A large parrot called out "Welcome to the zoo" from his left, while a solid-white peek-a-something glared at me like I wanted her lunch. Then I looked up and noticed two tiny, bright-orange feathery balls on his shoulder. They nuzzled his neck.

OMG. Cuteness overload.

"Most of the residents keep their distance, but these are the one we've trained to be held by guests. If you stretch out your arm, at least one of them will come to visit."

I did as instructed, and the white, snarky-looking

bird flapped onto my arm. I half expected her to peck my eyes out, but she simply scooted sideways up my arm until she found a comfortable spot. Donny pointed out a few special birds in the tangle above.

After a moment of nuzzling beaks and fluttering feathers, we moved on.

The building wound in a U shape connected by a narrow hallway at the U's bottom. The other side of the letter housed critters I wasn't sure I cared to see, but Donny insisted.

"We don't have to stay long, but I want you to see a few of the snakes—and their keepers."

"Their keepers?" I cocked my head.

He chuckled. "No cheating. Just wait. It'll be fun."

I couldn't decide if the mischief in his voice was more endearing or frightening. I chose to go with endearing because he was tall…and handsome…and his butt looked amazing in those jeans.

We rounded the bend and were greeted by a short, rail-thin guy with long, stringy hair I doubted had seen shampoo this decade. His grimy black hair blended into a black shirt that flowed down to even blacker pants. Beady eyes blinked in an odd, rapid rhythm as he looked up from one of the glass cases.

"Donald. Welcome. We are pleased to see you." His voice was metallic yet smooth—definitely spooky

—and he referred to himself in the plural, as if he were the Queen of England.

Donny grinned broadly and patted Mr. Munster on the shoulder. "Thanks, Edward. This is my friend, Michael. He's a virgin."

I nearly tripped. Both keepers chuckled.

"A *zoo* virgin. What did you think I meant?" Donny's grin held more of that mischief I'd seen earlier.

Before I could answer, Edward spoke. "Please forgive dear Donald. He has no manners, certainly not like our pretties here." He waved dramatically at the glass cages full of slithering bodies.

I suppressed a shiver, both at the snakes and their creepy caretaker.

Donny walked me quickly through the exhibit, and I was relieved when we stepped out into the sunlight and fresh air. There was something heavy about the air in that place. It felt, I don't know, *off*.

Maybe I just didn't like snakes.

"What did you think of Edward?" Donny asked as soon as we were out of earshot of the snake pen.

"Um, he was alright, I guess." I wasn't sure if they were friends or not and didn't want to offend Donny.

He laughed at my discomfort and leaned over, whispering, "He's fucking weird. I can see it all over your face—and you're right. He's nice enough, but he makes my skin crawl. It's like he came from House Slytherin, but creepier and without a shower."

"Yeah, I kept waiting for one of his *pretties* to poke its head out of his hair."

We shared a laugh, then he reached down, grabbed my hand, and pulled me forward. I felt a tingle travel up my arm at his touch. "Come on, you're gonna *love* this next family."

As we traveled along the path, hemmed in either side by the dock-like poles and heavy rope, a large grassy expanse opened on our left and I could see several varieties of antelope. Long, curved horns formed sharp points at the tip. Groups of ten or so moved in unison as they grazed lazily. The largest among them perked up as we passed, his head shooting straight up, horns high. There was a majestic beauty to the beast, a tranquility too.

A dozen paces later, another field opened to our right, but this one was more dirt than grass. It looked like it had been heavily trodden and barely a blade had survived. Donny's pace quickened and he called over his shoulder, "We're here."

He stopped in front of a large metal gate that led into a paddock. I didn't see any animals. Then the ground trembled. And again. If Donny hadn't been standing calmly nearby, I would've jumped back over the gate.

Seconds later, three mountains on legs appeared from nowhere. The elephants stood twice as tall as Donny, and must've weighed thousands of pounds. Wrinkles covered almost every inch of their bodies, and long tusks preceded them as they approached.

A man called out, "Hey, Donny. Come to see the fam?" His voice was warm and welcoming, and carried the same low rumble I heard in the beasts' thunderous footsteps.

One of the elephants moved away from the others, revealing a tall man with thick gray-black hair and a broad toothy smile. He waved at us, then issued a command to the elephants. On cue, all three animals stopped walking and turned to him, and one let out a deafening greeting.

Then the elephant trainer made a clicking sound and each member of his herd wrapped their trunks around him in a long, nasally hug. One of them got frisky and tickled his side with its snout. His high-pitched laughter was such a contrast from his booming voice that I couldn't help but join in his amusement. I caught Donny looking between the elephants and me, and his grin broadened. He was loving showing off his zoo as much as I was reveling in its wonders. I felt the warmth of his hand on my back as he urged me forward. "Come on, let's meet the family. The keeper's name is Ken."

We spent the next thirty minutes listening to Ken explain about the elephants, their upbringing, how they came to the zoo, what they ate and drank, the toys they played with—I didn't even know elephants played with toys. The handler's smile never wavered as he talked about each beast's unique personality, and he insisted I learn their names and call them properly.

Just when I thought we'd move on to the next exhibit, Donny pushed me into the middle of the elephants. He and Ken remained a few feet away, outside the ring of wrinkles. Ken issued a command and I received the same trunk-love they'd given him earlier. Rather than tickle me, Cootie, the female, used her snout to suck up my hair, then blow snot all over it.

Awesome. I was now the elephant version of Edward, the slimy-haired snake dude.

Then Ken whistled some other obscenity, and the elephants began walking in a ring around me. One minute they were creeping along, the next their tails were gripped by the trunk of the elephant to their rear, forming a solid circle. They walked faster and faster, kicking up dust and making the ground beneath me shake. As Cootie passed in front of me, I caught a flash of her eye and a quirk of her mouth.

Great. I've amused the snotty beast.

Donny giggled like a schoolgirl.

Ken hooted another directive and the circle froze. Each elephant dropped their partner's tail, took two steps backward, then reared up on their hind legs.

I'll admit it, I was terrified. I might've piddled a little.

Eight gazillion pounds of elephant was standing on two legs facing me from every direction. Their front legs wiggled wildly in the air, and the beasts roared. I later learned it was their version of a salute, a sort of primal welcome. At the time, I was worried about getting squished.

We thanked Ken, and I said goodbye, by name, to each of the powerful creatures. They really were gentle, and there was such intelligence in their eyes. I never would've expected it, but I could swear Cootie knew what I was saying. She wrapped her trunk around my neck and pulled me into a slobbery lick.

Yes, that was gross…and kind of cool.

We'd walked a few paces before I realized Donny had grabbed my hand and intertwined our fingers. He looked down at my slobber-covered face and squeezed my hand. A shiver thrilled up my arm again.

What was it with Donny making me shiver?

Without thinking, I returned his squeeze. I could see his cheeks tighten with his smile, though he didn't turn and look.

"What do you think so far?" he asked.

"This is so *awesome*. Thank you for sharing it with me. I had no idea Nashville had such an incredible zoo—or that I would love it so much."

"What do you think of the staff?"

I chuckled. "Well, as a wise man once told me, Edward is creepy as fuck. Ken is totally cool and laid-back, but has a hidden strength." I paused a moment. "It's like they're linked to their animals or something. That's so weird."

He nodded. "I wondered when you'd pick up on that. Most snake people are just like Edward. They dress like him, talk like him, even fail to bathe like him. I've been working in one zoo or another for nearly ten years, and they've all been basically the same. But elephant people are an interesting lot too."

"What do you mean?"

"Did you notice how many times Ken used the word *family*?"

"Huh. Yeah, now that you mention it. He did it a lot, even referred to the elephants as his family."

"You met Ken, the son. His parents are keepers here too. That's how elephant handlers are—*families* who go into the elephant-handling business. One family taking care of another—and they're very proud of that fact. Again, every zoo I've worked at, that's held true."

"Wow. That's…I don't know. Cool, I guess." I

thought a moment. "So, you're the cat guy. What are cat keepers like?"

He turned to face me with a glint in his eye, then took an aggressive step forward, so close our bodies pressed against each other, though our faces were still an inch or two apart. His voice was a low rumble full of passion and fire when he spoke. "Just wait. *My* family's next."

He ran a hand down my cheek and my whole body flared with heat.

WE FOLLOWED THE TRAIL FOR ANOTHER FIVE MINUTES before reaching a side entrance marked 'Employees Only.' I had noticed little change in the fields to our left and right, other than some barrier fencing made to look like natural obstacles. Interestingly, there were still no bars or cages. I thought zoos were covered in metal bars and wire mesh.

As we crossed a thin wooden bridge, I looked over the edge and realized why Nashville eschewed traditional enclosures. Rather than building fences to keep humans and animals separated, the clever zoo builders had dug moats some thirty feet deep and twenty feet wide. Looking out at the fields from the path, I could see there was a gap, but could not really understand the depth or purpose. From the sideways angle of the bridge, it was clear they were dug to divide the two worlds. It was an ingenious design that made it appear like guests were walking through the animals' habitat, rather than viewing them through prison bars. The idea was subtle, but the impact as a viewer was dramatic.

Donny sensed I'd stopped following and strode back to stand beside me on the bridge.

"Pretty cool, isn't it? There isn't a single place in the zoo where a guest sees a bar or metal cage. We want everything to look and feel as natural as possible."

I nodded, looking back down into the gulf between field and path. "What if one of the animals got down there somehow? How would you get it out? And what would stop it from climbing up the other side?"

"They do occasionally get brave and stray too close to the edge. There are a few openings at various points of the gully where we can let them back into their living area. As for climbing up the other side, there are electrified wires, starting about ten feet from the top, that ensure they don't get all the way up. The zaps aren't strong enough to hurt them, but they sure scare the shit out of them enough to change their mind about getting out."

Again, the design impressed me.

Donny grabbed my hand again and pulled me off the bridge. "Come on, this is what I really wanted to show you today."

We rounded the corner and were met by a wall of thick metal bars, the first I'd seen since we entered the zoo—aside from those at the front gate to keep unwanted humans out when the park was closed. The bars formed a box, with more bars crisscrossing the top. I looked through to find the box situated directly against one of the moats that separated two exhibits. There was a thin dirt bridge, barely as wide as a gymnast's balance beam, leading from the exhibit on the far side into the cage.

Donny pressed his face between two of the bars and made a whirring sound. It undulated between high and low pitches in a rhythm that was somehow familiar, though I couldn't place where I'd heard it before. In seconds, a blur of orange, black, and white crossed the bridge and skidded to a stop before the bars where Donny's head still protruded.

He never flinched. I nearly jumped out of my jeans.

A massive Bengal tiger, with a head twice the width of Donny's, peered up, sniffed the air, then pressed its head against Donny's forehead. I watched in amazement as the tiger closed its eyes and emitted a deep rumble. I didn't speak tiger; I wasn't sure if it was happy or hungry.

Donny then made a low *guff-guff* sound that started deep in his throat and rose to his lips, though they never parted. In response, the tiger mimicked the sound loudly and switched from a head-nuzzle to licking his face. If it wasn't for the beast's size, its licking and nuzzling was like the reaction of any common house cat when greeting their chosen human.

I was transfixed.

Then it hit me. Donny's head was pressed through the bars against a massive predator with sharp, pointy teeth and even pointier claws. That cat could've crushed his skull like a watermelon.

Sorry for the imagery there. That was kinda gross.

Before I could react or pull him to safety, or whatever stupid thing I was thinking at the time, Donny straightened and turned toward me.

"Come meet Tina. I hand-raised her from a cub. She was three weeks old when she came to live in my house."

My jaw must've dropped, or my face made some other cartoonish effect, because he barked a laugh. "Trust me. Tina knows me as her father, as any cat would know the human who raised them. If I approve of you, she will too."

"Uh, okay. Cool. Right. Uh…sure."

I was articulate as ever—and utterly unconvinced —but Donny's broad smile reached well into his deep brown eyes, and I couldn't resist his outstretched hand.

Shit, that tiger was big, and her teeth looked like small, curved white daggers.

When I was close enough, he took my hand and held it out before Tina's nose. Her eyes snapped up to Donny's, then narrowed slightly and shifted toward mine. Her gaze wasn't exactly hostile, but I wasn't sure she fully appreciated my presence either. Could tigers be jealous? What if she didn't want to share her human, her father?

Without relinquishing her protective position between us, she leaned her nose toward my hand and sniffed. Her eyes flickered back to Donny with one last question, then I *felt* her relax as she nuzzled my hand with the top of her head. Her rumbling purr vibrated up my arm.

Donny squeezed my shoulder and I released the breath I'd been holding. "She likes you," he said, a proud smile curling his lips.

"I'm glad *you* can tell. I had images of my fingers being ripped off and blood spurting all over your pretty blond hair."

He leaned down and pressed his forehead into

mine, similar to how he'd greeted Tina. "I'm glad you survived, digits intact."

Then he laughed and stepped back, amused at his own jackass-ness.

I couldn't help but laugh too. It was a relief. Then I realized my hand was still on the head of a six-hundred-pound tiger. The only movement Tina had made was to lean *into* my touch. Maybe he was right and she *did* like me.

Then she pulled back and sneezed. Snot and spittle flew all over me, coating my hand in slime. Donny lost all composure, doubling in laughter before giving in to gravity and sitting on the grassy ground.

"Thanks a lot," I said to Tina. "What is it with me and the animals here blowing their noses on me?"

She blinked up at me, wiped her face with a paw, then craned her neck forward and licked the goo off my hand. My eyes popped wide as she gently cleaned every drop.

When I turned back to Donny, his eyes were equally wide. "Huh. She really does like you. Cats don't clean others they don't like. That's her way of apologizing for the snot, and saying she accepts you. It's a very intimate gesture I wouldn't have expected for months, if ever."

My chest puffed out. *Damn, I'm good. Like effin' Siegfried and that other guy good.*

In that moment of triumph, Tina gave me a playful nip. I yanked my hand back and let out the manliest squeal any tiger had ever heard.

Donny roared, and I swear that Tina laughed along with him. She let out a gurgling sound and her eyes turned to slits while the skin around her nose crinkled.

Damned cat.

When everyone had finished their cawing and crinkling at my expense, Donny rose and gripped my shoulders. His hands were what you'd expect on a six-four dude, thick with a wide span. His grasp was firm. He leaned into me and my heart raced as his breath tickled my nose. His lips pressed into mine. They were chapped and rough, yet somehow felt right on this strong keeper of beasts. He held me for a long moment, then pulled back and smiled again.

Tina growled, shattering the dizzying moment.

Donny released my shoulders and turned back to the cat, placing both hands on either side of her broad face. He scratched behind her ears with his fingers, and she emitted that whirring rumble again and leaned into his caress. They touched foreheads one last time.

"We can't go in there, unfortunately."

I raised a brow, unsure if I *wanted* to go in there. Tina accepting me through iron bars was one thing, but roaming into her territory was a completely different form of terror.

He grinned, reading my thoughts yet again. "She'd never *intentionally* hurt me, but think about playing with a house cat. Sometimes they get a little too rough and draw blood with their teeth or claws. They're just playing, but they get carried away. Now, replace that three-pound cat with Miss Tina's six hundred pounds."

"Right. No playing on Tina's turf. Definitely okay with that." I thought a moment. "You said she lived with you? You mean *actually* lived with you in your home? Like a house cat?"

"Yeah, that's what hand-raised means. The idea is to get the cats used to the person who will be their ultimate keeper, and to humans in general. They learn smells, tastes, sounds. Most importantly, they learn trust. There's a bond between a hand-raised cat and their handler that doesn't exist with any other keeper–animal relationship. It's special."

Why did my heart soar hearing him talk about hand-raising a cat?

His eyes drifted somewhere else as he spoke, and his smile transformed from playful to wistful. I could see him replaying memories of Tina in his home, of her as a cub nestling on his bed or in his lap.

Wait, I was not thinking about his bed—*or his lap*. I swear. We'd never talked about his bed. I'd never seen it. Really, his bed had never popped into my head.

Damn it. Now I couldn't get his bed—*or his lap*—out of my mind.

That's *your* fault!

"Did you go somewhere?" he asked.

I shook my head free of beds and laps. "No, was just imagining Tina as a cub. I bet she was adorable."

"She was just a ball of the softest fur you've ever felt. Her eyes had opened the week before I got her, but she still couldn't see very well, and she stumbled around more than walked. I bottle-fed her for over a month." I watched him drift away again. "Tigers basically sleep all the time as cubs, only waking to eat, drink, or poop. They're not really playful like other cats. She slept in my arms or lap more hours than I could count, and I loved every minute of it." He closed his eyes. "I can still feel her purr against my chest."

Tina must've sensed he was talking about her, because she let out a low growl-purr and scratched herself against the bars. Donny gave her a deep scratch, earning an even louder rumble.

We were standing in a zoo in the middle of Nashville, but I felt like I'd been transported to another planet. It's not like we went to Africa or anything exotic, but seeing all this through Donny's eyes was extraordinary. These cats were family to him in a way I'd never understood or expected. I would've thought keepers were professionals trained to feed and care for animals, but hand-raising and soul-stirring bonds? This was something special, and I was honored to witness it.

"How long did she live with you?" I asked.

"We judge that more by size and weight than time. Cats grow within a range, but can also vary widely in when they reach puberty or other key physical markers. They normally stay with us until they're around a hundred pounds, maybe a little more. A lot of that depends on breed and temperament. Our zoo gives me a lot of discretion, while others have hard rules forcing a keeper to relinquish an animal at certain weights."

"Sounds like letting them go would be hard."

"It is and it isn't. I miss having her at home, but she wasn't comfortable there anymore. She needed room to roam and hunt, to be the majestic beast she was born to be. She couldn't do that in a house or apartment. Plus, I knew all along that I'd be her keeper, so it's not like I lost her. Our living arrangement was all that really changed."

He guided me back to the main path where we wound our way around the zoo.

"Is Tina the only cat you've hand-raised?"

"No, she's my third, and I have a few other friends living with me right now."

Interesting. There was mischief in his voice, but he didn't elaborate.

We turned onto another side path and came to another box, this one with solid metal walls and bars on the front face. It was a sturdier version of the cage I'd met Tina in. On the far side was a series of two sliding panels that allowed keepers to bring in one animal at a time while closing the other panel behind them, reminding me of an entrance to a restaurant in some wintery city where you entered one door, then another as the first closed, to keep the cold out.

Donny walked up to a series of buttons that rose along the left edge of the cage and pressed the blue one. A horn sounded for as long as his thumb kept pressure on the button; a few seconds. I heard thunder as heavy paws carried something large toward the cage. Satisfied his call had been answered, Donny lifted a plastic cover and pressed a red button. It looked like the zookeeper's version of launching a nuclear missile. The nerd in me thought it was *totally cool*.

A second later, the panel facing the living area opened and a blur of tan raced in. A yellow button was pressed next to close the outer panel, then open the inner one. The mechanism timed those actions so two panels were never opened at the same time. As soon as the inner panel lifted, powerful golden eyes surveyed the cage and the lustrous mane of a male lion shook, heralding the beast's arrival. The moment the powerful cat strode into the cage, the inner panel slammed shut, triggered by a motion sensor I hadn't noticed.

The lion padded its way toward us, and I took an involuntary step back.

Donny didn't approach like he had with Tina.

When the lion was a foot from the bars, he sat on his hindquarters and looked expectantly up at Donny. His head was wider than my shoulders, and rose to Donny's chest when seated. Standing, he was monstrous. Behind his thick mane, the fur on his body laid back like a short-haired house cat, in shimmering tan waves. I could see muscles ripple every time he moved.

"Uh, Donny, that's a freakin' lion."

"You're *good*, practically an expert now," he teased.

I rolled my eyes. "Thanks, Obi Wan. What the hell are we doing with a lion? You're not going to cuddle with that thing, are you?"

"No. No cuddling Duke. I didn't hand-raise him, and lions can be less predictable than tigers, especially when it's feeding time. We're just going to give him what he wants."

"That doesn't involve a Michael sacrifice, does it?"

He ignored my jibe and walked around the side of the solid wall, returning with a bucket.

"I had Duke's keeper leave us his dinner so you could experience feeding time. Care to help?" The mischief was back in his eyes again.

"Uh, sure."

He reached into the bucket and pulled out a slab of some kind of bloody meat on a bone. It could've been remains of the aforementioned keeper, or maybe one of the antelopes I'd seen earlier—I couldn't tell. I didn't care. It dripped and oozed all over the ground, and Duke responded immediately, sniffing the air and pacing in front of the bars. He huffed excitedly.

Great. Get the lion all worked up. That's *exactly* what I hoped for.

Donny grinned as I squirmed, then tossed the gooey mass between the bars. Duke lunged. The sound of rending flesh and crunching bones echoed inside the metal box. One chomp of his mighty jaws shattered the femur that was thicker than my arm into a dozen splinters. Duke downed the smaller pieces, while larger bones fell near his paws.

When he had finished his appetizer and was again

facing us, seated and staring, Donny held the bucket toward me.

"Your turn, Great Lion Tamer."

I looked down and another bone-in-rib-something poked up from a disgusting pool of blood that filled half the pail. I'd never been squeamish, but that was gross, and I really didn't want to touch it. Unfortunately, a guy I wanted to impress was standing there, waiting.

I realized just then that I *really* wanted to impress him. Interesting.

I did the manliest two-fingered grip I could muster and plucked the thick slab of bony meat out. Blood and gore splashed everywhere. Lovely. When I looked up, Duke was standing with his nose just outside the bars, his golden eyes fixed on me and the main course dripping in my hand—or did he think *I* was his main course? I didn't want to find out.

I flung the bloody hunk toward the cage and Duke swatted it down with a massive paw through the bars, then dragged his prize inside.

If I thought my heart had raced when Donny kissed me, it was running sprints right then.

Holy king of the beasts.

We watched Duke finish his lunch, then Donny reversed the button-pressing procedure to return him to the living area. For his part, Duke knew the routine and didn't argue when the metal slider lifted. He simply turned and strode through.

"They've each been trained since they were juveniles to follow this feeding ritual. They know exactly what the horns and sliding doors mean, and what's expected. On the off-chance they balk, we have prods to help them remember what to do." He pointed around the corner to a sealed plastic case mounted to the outer wall of the cage.

Once Duke was secured and the cage was reset, Donny rummaged through a metal cabinet next to the plastic container and returned with a towel. I wiped a few blood splashes and the last of Tina's slobber from my arms. He chuckled as I scrubbed at dried snot.

An hour later, we'd returned to the zoo's main entrance, having walked a complete circle around the sprawling park. Donny turned to me before unlocking the metal gate that led to the parking lot. "What did you think? Was it alright?"

"Yeah, I guess, if you're into that sort of thing." I tried playing it cool, but the twelve-year-old in me couldn't resist. "What are you talking about? That was the coolest, most exciting, craziest day I've had in forever. It was a total blast. Thank you so much. You have the coolest job ever."

Donny broke into warm laughter. His smile… wow. His smile made me swoon. He was the most beautiful cat I'd seen all day, and it was only in that moment that I realized how much I liked him.

"Can I see you again?" he asked. "I'd really like to. It might be nice to get another kiss sometime too."

Sweet baby Jesus, he sounded like a man from one of those old-timey movies asking if he could court me. Despite the blood, snot, and dust that covered us both, it might've been the most romance-novel-worthy thing anyone had ever said to me.

"I'd like that. Both. I mean, yes, I'd like you to see me, or me see you. Again. And the kiss. Yes. Well, shit. Yes to all of it. Yes!"

I really was sputtering by the end of…whatever that was.

He beamed. He leaned down and planted another kiss on my lips as his hand pressed gently against the side of my head. Strong fingers raked through my hair until he held my neck, pulling me into him.

I thought I might pass out.

15

WHO YOU BE?

Donny called the next day. I snorted when he said Tina couldn't stop talking about me. He said she'd growled and paced back and forth until he assured her he'd ask me out again. He'd kept a straight face—well, a straight voice—throughout the whole tale, and that had made it irresistibly cute. I found myself grinning so wide my cheeks hurt by the time we'd hung up.

April's on-again, off-again warmth and rain, coupled with waves of pollen that knocked my sinuses into the last decade, gave each day an odd bipolar mix of pleasure and pain. Now that basketball season was over, and the rush of AAU and summer leagues had yet to arrive, I had little to occupy my evenings.

As we learned before, boredom is a dangerous thing.

I threw myself into working out, and my shoulders rounded and chest filled out. T-shirts that had hung loosely last year now fit snugly, and the sleeves strained at their hems from my growing arms. I'd never known the feeling of a healthy, growing body before. It was a rush—and not just the post-workout, endorphin-fueled rush guys talk about experiencing after a hard day with weights. It was the mental fix that came with looking in the mirror in the morning and realizing I was no longer a bean pole. The definition forming between my biceps and triceps was exciting, something I'd seen on the muscle heads at the gym and longed for.

I was, by no man's definition, a muscle head, but I was able to change my *body type* answer on my AOL profile from thin to athletic. I stared at the screen, watching the cursor blink as it waited for me to hit *confirm*, struggling to believe I was about to enter the world of athletic-bodied men. For a second, I wondered if changing that answer would impact the guys who'd be willing to respond when I messaged them. Did I need new pictures?

Hell yes I did! Before pressing the button, I raced to my closet and threw on a blue tank top that fit just right, meaning it was a size too small. Everything looked bigger in that tank top. I loved it. Then I dug in my dresser drawer for my digital camera.

Yes, kids, this was before phones had cameras. In fact, it was before cell phones were even a thing. Don't pass out.

A hundred shots later, I was satisfied with how the light from my bedroom window created shadows in the creases in my arms and across my chest.

Yes, it was a vain moment. Give me a break.

I hit *cancel* on my profile update, uploaded the new photos, then reupdated my profile with the new *athletic* body type.

Ding. An instant message window popped up.

That was odd. I wasn't in a chat room, and none of the guys on my handy friends list were online. Who could be ringing my bell?

I giggled at the song that started in my head and danced a bad white-man jig in my office chair.

RAL1027: HEY

Huh. RAL1027, wonder what that means. I sifted through my printed profile sheets, now neatly alphabetized, hole-punched, and bound in a three-ring binder.

Don't make fun. I had to keep track somehow.

MICHAELSPORTSGUY: HI. SORRY, HAVE WE CHATTED BEFORE?

RAL1027: NO. SAW YOUR PROFILE AND THOUGHT I'D SAY HI.

MichaelSportsGuy: Ok. Cool. Hi. I'm Michael.

RAL1027: Ryan.

MichaelSportsGuy: Nice to meet ya, Ryan.

RAL1027: You too.

There was a long enough pause at this point, so I got up, went to the kitchen, and made a bowl of cereal. When I came back, Ryan had responded a few times.

RAL1027: Whatcha up to?

RAL1027: Still there?

RAL1027: Hey, gotta run. Check your email. Sent you a pic. Feel free to return.

On a whim, I added him to my friends list. The window said he was no longer online, so, between bites of Frosted Flakes, I clicked my email and opened his pic. Blond, gray eyes, nice smile, fit from what I could tell. The pic looked like one taken for work, a headshot that only went to his shoulders and revealed nothing more than his light-blue dress shirt.

Didn't this guy know he was supposed to send a shirtless pic so I could judge if he was worthy or not? Wasn't that the rule? AOL was a fairly new invention, but I was sure the Gay Handbook covered the topic.

Before shutting down my computer, I printed Ryan's profile and picture, then smacked it through the three-hole punch. I scribbled a note on his page, then put two stars at the top. No circle. The conversation was too brief to earn the highest distinction available.

16

LIQUID DIET

Date night came quickly. As I rummaged for clean clothes, a task more challenging than I'd expected, my excitement grew. I couldn't remember a day more fun than the one we'd spent at the zoo, certainly not in a long time. Who gets to pet tigers on a date? I didn't know Donny well, but there was something in his childlike smile that made me want to spend more time with him.

I found a clean shirt, but sighed as I realized how badly wrinkled it had become hidden in the clean pile all week.

Yes, I know, I should've laid my clothes out when they were still warm from the dryer. Better yet, I should've put them away. Stop nagging.

I was waiting for the iron to heat up when the phone rang. I banged my shin on the coffee table sprinting across the room, but managed to grab the receiver before the caller hung up. "Hello?"

"Please don't hate me."

"Donny?"

"Yep. It's me. I'm really sorry to do this, but I need to put off our dinner. The bar called and two guys called out sick. They need me to work tonight after all."

"Well, that sucks," I blurted without thinking. "I mean, I'm sorry they're sick. We'll have to pick another night."

I could swear I heard him let out a breath.

"We definitely will. How about I cook for you to make up for it? I make a mean pasta."

"Perfect-o," I said with a terrible Italian accent. He chuckled.

"Hey, since you don't have plans now, why don't you stop by the bar? I know a guy who's stuck working you might like."

I grinned and played along. "Really? What's he look like? I'm pretty picky these days."

"Well, he's not much to look at, but he works out, and I hear he's great with cats."

"Awesome," I feigned sarcasm. "You're setting me up with a crazy cat lady. Are you sure this dude's not a lesbian in disguise?"

He snorted. "Definitely not a lesbian. Although, he

does go to Home Depot a lot. Is that a coincidence?"

We both laughed.

"What time do you work?"

"I'm headed in now. With two men down, they'll need help to set up."

"Alright. I'll grab something to eat and head over in a couple hours. Look forward to seeing you…I mean, Crazy Kitty Man."

He snorted again. "See you soon."

I hung up the phone, disappointed that dinner had been scrapped, but excited he still wanted to spend time together. I'd been blown off before, and this was definitely not a blow-off. On a whim, I dialed Dwayne. "Hey, are you working tonight? Donny had to work at the bar and asked me to swing by. You should come."

"As it turns out, I got cut tonight. Want a dinner date since yours canceled?"

"You're the best date ever. Absolutely!"

Thirty minutes later, Dwayne and I sat staring at plates piled high with rotisserie chicken, fried okra, and mashed potatoes. He looked suspiciously at the okra, but I was in heaven. What can I say, my mama raised a veggie-lovin' Southern boy.

We bantered like the two old guys in the balcony on *The Muppet Show*. Dwayne was the best friend I could ever hope to have. He grounded me. Somehow, he never took himself—or me—too seriously. Time with him was comfortable and safe, and I knew he'd be there no matter what insanity I got myself into.

Everyone needs a Dwayne.

An hour later, we strode into the Chute. There were several guys seated around the bar, and Donny was bouncing quickly between them, filling glasses and chatting. Our two regular stools stood empty, one with a Jack and Coke beside a tumbler filled with limes. A second glass with Coke fizzed nearby.

"How did he know we'd be here now?" Dwayne whispered to me.

I shrugged and grinned at Donny's thoughtfulness. My chest warmed as the tall man behind the bar turned and waved. His smile lit up the dim room.

Dwayne's elbow jabbed my ribs. "Are you going to stand here in the doorway grinning like an idiot, or can we go see him now?"

"Oh, sorry. Sure. Let's go."

Donny leaned over and hugged Dwayne in greeting, then did the same with me. He squeezed my back with his hands and pressed a kiss into my cheek before pulling away.

I flushed and grinned stupidly again.

A guy on the other side of the bar turned to his neighbor and said, "Looks like somebody's taken Donny off the market."

I nearly fell off my stool.

"You okay?" Donny asked, either not hearing or ignoring the comment.

"Yeah, sorry. Just missed the stool."

Dwayne eyed me with a wry grin. When Donny turned to serve another customer, he leaned over and whispered, "You really like him, don't you?"

"I…uh…sure. I guess so. He's super nice, and the zoo date was one of the best ever—and not just because of the animals. He was awesome too. I definitely want to get to know him better."

"And you want to find out if *everything* is as big as the rest of him too. I know you."

"Dwayne!" I feigned offense. "I'm a gentleman. I have no idea what you're talking about."

He guffawed. "You know *exactly* what I'm talking about. Besides, I'm curious too. I bet that thing's huge. It might even give your tight little ass a run for your money."

Now I *was* blushing. "My ass—"

"Go on. Don't stop for me," Donny said, leaning over with his chin in both hands, elbows on the bar, batting innocent eyelashes at me.

Eight shades of red turned into twenty. I wanted to crawl under the bar. "Uh…Dwayne was just…I mean—"

"I was agreeing with Michael that your ass looks good in those jeans," Dwayne interjected.

I turned, eyes wide, and slapped him playfully on the arm. "I didn't say—"

"So you don't like my ass in these jeans?" Donny asked, clearly picking a side.

"No, I didn't say that—"

"So you *do* like his ass?" Dwayne countered.

I felt like a tennis ball at Wimbledon. Just when I thought I was safely across the net, someone smacked me back to the other side—and those damned royals did *nothing* to stop it, just sat in their fancy nest and watched.

Unable to string two words together, I grabbed my Coke and took a long pull.

Dwayne and Donny shared a grin while I drank. Donny turned, slapped one of his butt cheeks loudly, then crossed the bar to refill someone else's drink.

Dwayne was hyperventilating.

"Thanks a lot. Some wing man you are," I groused, unwilling to admit how funny the scene had actually been.

Dwayne stood and pointed at the restroom. He couldn't speak through the tears. His shoulders never stopped quaking as he laughed all the way to the far side of the bar.

"He's a good friend, isn't he?"

I turned back to find Donny leaning over the counter again. "I hate to admit it, but he's the best."

He chuckled. "Those are rare. I had one like him." His eyes shifted from laughter to—something.

"Had?"

He nodded slowly. "Yeah. He took two bullets."

"Bullets?"

"Yeah, we served together." His voice stilled.

I watched as he drifted far away, staring at the counter before him. His brow furrowed, and his eyes closed. I wanted to say something, but no words could bring his friend back, and they certainly wouldn't be worthy of honoring his memory, however well intentioned.

A pair of guys entering the bar brought Donny back to the present. He gave me a long look, then nodded and turned back to his work. I wasn't sure what had passed between us, but I was sure *something* had. I got the impression he didn't tell many people about his time overseas. Given what he'd lost, I couldn't blame him.

"Penny."

I looked up to find Dwayne settling back onto his stool, staring at me. I raised a questioning brow.

"For your thoughts. You look lost in them."

"Oh yeah. Donny just told me some things…from his past."

"His time in the army?"

I looked up, surprised.

"I've been coming here a long time. Sometimes he wears dog tags. On nights when he works without a shirt, they're hard to miss. He's never talked about them, but I could tell they weren't the kind you buy in a gift shop."

"How do you know the difference?"

He cocked his head. "Because I was in the navy. And because of the way he'd hold them when he thought no one was watching. I could just tell."

"You never told me you were in the navy. When?"

"A lifetime ago." Now Dwayne got that same faraway look in his eyes. "I'll tell you about it sometime, just not here, not now. Okay?"

"Sure," I said quietly.

The slow trickle of men entering the bar had turned into a full-on flood, and Donny was struggling to keep up, bouncing from one waving hand demanding alcohol to the next. He stole a moment to apologize for ignoring us.

"It's alright," I said. "We know you have to work. Why don't we go and let you do your thing?"

Donny leaned over and kissed me full on the mouth. Conversations around the bar hushed. Then everyone applauded and cheered as he pulled back. I turned crimson, earning a chorus of giggles from the gaggle. "Dinner Sunday night? I definitely won't work then, no matter who's sick."

I grinned, overcoming my embarrassment. "Kissing like that? How can I say no?"

Another wild cheer erupted around us. Dwayne ushered me out before my ears could turn any redder.

17

A COMPLETELY DIFFERENT ZOO

As I pulled into Donny's driveway, a whole zoo's worth of butterflies took flight in my chest.

I no longer wore the label *newborn gay*, having been on a number of dates and locked down my first boyfriend, even if that was only for a few months. I'd made meaningful, intimate love to a man I cared for deeply. And I'd been tied to bedposts with silk bonds.

No, I was definitely not new anymore.

That still didn't make me experienced. One boyfriend and one breakup hadn't turned me jaded or stolen my idealism. I still believed in The Dream. You know, that sappy daydream where I'd meet the perfect man, fall helplessly in love, then walk down the aisle together while rose petals and doves flew overhead.

Wait, doves poop, don't they? Scratch the doves.

Insert Disney movie music. Or Journey—*definitely* Journey. They were my all-time favorite band. I needed them on my special day.

Stop laughing. It's an awesome dream—if a bit sappy—and I still believe in it whether you do or not.

Where were we? Oh, driveway. Right.

I stared through the windshield at Donny's house. It was a nice starter home, a one-story brick box that probably had two or three bedrooms and an outdated kitchen. The neighborhood was nice too. Cars and trucks filled the driveways on either side, giving the impression this was a middle-class working neighborhood, exactly where I envisioned a zookeeper might live.

Sitting there, my mind strayed to our date at the zoo. That day had been such an incredible surprise. There was no way a simple dinner without animals or snakes could top that.

Well, unless he *actually* topped that.

My butt quivered at the thought.

I hopped out of the car and strode up to the house. With a couple taps of the clacker, Donny appeared, his towering frame consuming the doorway. He wore tan shorts and a light-blue shirt. For a moment, I thought he was still in his zoo uniform. He definitely looked like a hot park ranger, with thick, hairy legs and broad shoulders. Then he smiled, and I swooned.

"Hey you." He opened the door and wrapped me in a tight hug while planting a long kiss on my lips. I don't know what I expected from his greeting, but it wasn't *that*. I melted in his arms. When he pulled back, still holding me, his eyes sparkled, the tiny creases around them curling upward in a smile all their own.

Sweet buttery popcorn. My heart fluttered again.

"Come on. I need your help with something while I finish dinner."

Curious, I let him take my hand and lead me through his house, which was exactly what I had pictured while sitting in the driveway. Paneled walls and fixtures from the '70s surrounded us. A few pictures of tigers and lions hung on the walls, some with Donny, others without.

We came to a closed door, and he turned to face me. "I need you to babysit for me. Are you okay with that?"

Babysit? What the hell? He never mentioned having kids.

Wait. I *loved* kids. Was he serious? Another swoon threatened, but I slapped that bitch back into place and stared up at my host. "Uh, sure. Whatever you need."

"Alright. Stay here a second. Let me get every-thing ready."

Um. That's weird. Did he have his child in a cage? Was this about to turn into one of those shows where the police rescue a dozen kidnap victims who'd been hidden behind walls?

"Okay, come on in." He sounded amused, not what I expected from a serial kidnapper.

I pushed open the door, revealing a small, unfur-nished bedroom. A twin-sized mattress lay on the floor, and a large metal cage rested against the far wall. Donny sat with his legs crossed in the middle of the room, his back facing me.

"Shut the door behind you."

I complied.

"Now come sit with us."

Us? Oh shit.

I squatted on the floor and he turned, holding a squirming ball of pure-white fluff. He held the ball up and four paws flopped to its side. Wide golden eyes stared up at me.

"This is Roxy, our newest Bengal tiger cub." He held her out and I took her in my arms, cradling her like a baby. Her fur was softer than any puppy I'd ever petted. Her eyes held a lazy, disinterested look, and her body oozed into my lap as though she had no bones. I scratched her head and was rewarded with a rumble far bigger than the tiny body in my arms should've been able to produce.

I couldn't stop smiling. Roxy was adorable.

"She won't play or anything. At this age, what you see is what you get. She barely gets excited at feeding time. Sometimes I think she gets annoyed I'm interrupting her sleep to feed her." He chuckled.

"She's beautiful."

"Yeah, she really is. Her markings won't show for another couple months. This solid-white stage is my favorite. I'll only get to keep her for another three or four months. Bengals grow really fast."

"I don't know how you give them up. I'm already falling for this little girl."

He grinned. "It can be hard sometimes."

Hee hee, he said hard, the little devil whispered in my head.

"Let's put her to bed. She's not who I need you to watch."

This dinner date just got really interesting. I could hardly wait to see what he had in the other bedrooms.

Hey, stop that. I was thinking about furry, cuddly things.

No, not *that* furry thing, you filthy-minded beast!

Once Roxy was secured in her crate, we moved down the hallway to bedroom number two. This time we entered together, though he insisted I close my eyes and sit on the floor.

A second later, a knobby, furry head slammed into my chest, and my eyes flew open to find a football-sized cougar cub playfully pouncing into me. A blur of motion to my right revealed a brother or sister racing around to attack from the side. They were young, only a couple months old, but keen intelligence showed in their eyes as they coordinated their approach. I couldn't stop laughing.

And then stinker number three pounced on my back.

I hadn't seen nor heard the other cub sneak around my left side while number two distracted me. The pounce caught me completely by surprise. Tiny needles poked into my back as the assailant climbed up to nibble my neck.

Donny stood in the corner of the room, laughing at my dilemma.

"These are the three troublemakers I wanted you to meet. That's Simon in your lap, Alvin crawling up your right arm, and Theo on your back."

I barked a laugh. "Those are chipmunks, not cougars."

"Yeah, I know, but zookeepers have a sense of humor too. Besides, we run out of names and have to get creative." He tussled my hair as he walked toward the door, careful not to dislodge any of the cubs. "I'm going to work on dinner. Good luck."

Just like that, the door clicked shut and the cubs renewed their attack, playfully pawing and gnawing like the baby cats they were. I was amazed at how they communicated on some instinctual level, coordinating their efforts. Every time I'd get the upper hand, they'd retreat to the far side of the room and glare, then Simon would stalk toward me, his eyes never leaving mine. Simon was the instigator, the bait. Alvin was the muscle, blundering in whenever Simon's devious dance had me mesmerized. Theo was the assassin, the ninja.

The other two cats were smart, but Theo was brilliant. At one point, I picked him up and he chomped down on my hand. I let out a yelp. He released me immediately and looked up with his ears pinned back, then carefully craned his neck to lick the skin his teeth had just pierced, his version of an apology for playing too roughly.

Alvin let me hold him upside down and scratch his belly. His tiny purr was more akin to a pull-cord lawnmower starting than any cat's purr I'd heard, but I loved it. He wrapped his paws around my non-scratching fingers and pulled them into him as I worked. His mouth held an upward turn I took for a smile, as his eyes lolled back in his head in pure ecstasy.

Our moment of bliss lasted as long as it took the other two minions to get a drink and come up with a new plan. I chuckled as Theo snuck around behind me again.

"You know I can see you, right?"

He squinted his eyes in concentration, unwilling to let my teasing distract from his mission. Meanwhile, Simon pranced innocently toward me, climbed onto my lap, giving Alvin a lick on the head. My mower's engine grew louder at his brother's touch.

In a feat of magical synchronization, Theo and Simon leapt at the same moment, one pouncing on my chest, the other my back, but I was ready for them this time. I grabbed Simon, tickling his toothpick-like ribs. He squirmed and squealed, finally freeing himself and sprinting across the room to the safety of their crate.

Theo climbed my back again, locking his teeth onto my hair and yanking. I shook my head and the rascal dropped free, then bolted around for a frontal assault.

Thirty minutes flew by, and the tiny terrors never tired.

When Donny returned, he had to detach the chipmunks one at a time. As soon as he got one, the other two latched on. It was a losing battle. They squirmed and let out the cutest growls, clearly not done with play time. I wasn't sure I wanted to stop either. That was the most fun I'd had since our day at the zoo—and that day ranked on my all-time list.

Resigned to plan B, Donny grabbed a bottle full of milk I hadn't noticed and handed it to me. He then grabbed two others and shook them in front of the cougars. The change was instant. They swarmed the bottles, tiny pink tongues lolling and licking.

Simon chose me. I guessed all that climbing and attacking had bonded us. He lay peacefully on his stomach in my lap while I bottle-fed him like an infant. As his brother had done earlier, he gripped my off-hand with his paws and held it as he drank. Every time he looked up at me and blinked, my heart skipped a beat.

I was so wrapped up in watching Simon feed that I'd almost forgotten Donny and the others were in the room. He was staring at me, smiling, when I looked up. "What?"

"You're a natural. They adore you."

My eyes drifted back to Simon. "I'm kinda falling for them too."

"Just them?"

My breath caught. If you didn't count the bar visits, we'd only been on two real dates, and I hardly knew how to respond. I was definitely drawn to him though.

I gave him a sheepish look. "The keeper's not too bad once you get to know him."

He must've liked that answer because he leaned over and planted a kiss on me that nearly made me drop my pussy.

Cat! Pussy *cat*, you rogue!

18

REPORTING IN, SIR

"**W**ait. You've had *three* dates and been to visit him at the bar *four* times?" Jason asked.

I shrugged. "Yeah. Maybe five times at the bar."

"The staff knows him by name, but they call him Donny's boy." Dwayne smirked.

"I can't help it if people like me."

Jason wouldn't be thrown off the scent. "Don't distract me. That's *eight* dates. You went to his bar specifically to see him. On more than one occasion, he *invited* you. Those count as dates."

"And?" I had no idea where this was going.

"And you haven't seen him naked yet? What kind of self-respecting homosexual are you?"

"Apparently, one with more self-respect than the slut grilling him at the moment," I shot back.

Dwayne choked on his coffee.

"Said the guy who bedded a sky mattress without getting his name, then became a couple sandwich because someone dangled a hot dog…I mean, hot tub…in front of him."

"Hey! It was a *nice* hot tub, and we actually used it."

"You used the hot dog too," Dwayne said.

Jason spat tea all over the table.

"Ha ha. Very funny." I crossed my arms. "I don't know why we haven't done more than make out. We just haven't. The zoo wasn't really the place to get naked, and when I had dinner at his place, he didn't invite me to stay. We cuddled on the couch and kissed, but that was it."

"Maybe he's heard about your deviant ways?" Jason jabbed.

"Or maybe he's a gentleman and wants to get to know me before we bump and grind," I countered.

"How do you know who bumps and who grinds? Have you even talked about sex?" Jason asked.

I thought a moment, realizing we hadn't. What surprised me more was that I didn't care the subject hadn't come up. I just enjoyed being with him. "We talked about pretty heavy stuff the other night. He told me about his family, then talked about—"

"What?" Jason pressed.

"…His time in the service."

Dwayne leaned in. "You don't have to talk about that if it's too personal. Those are his truths to share, not yours."

"I know," I snapped, more defensively than intended. I sucked in a breath. "I know. It was just tough for him to open up, and I was surprised he did. I'm sure there's plenty he didn't tell me, but he described a lot, including how he lost his best friend."

"Jesus," Jason said.

"I wanted to hold him, comfort him, not jump his bones. If it's right, all that will come in time. I'm honestly enjoying just getting to know him."

"He is setting a high bar for dates. Shit. Who's ever going to top the zoo or wrestling with baby cougars?"

I giggled. "You said *top*."

Jason giggled along with me as Dwayne rolled his eyes and took another sip of coffee.

"So, I hear he actually is a top, and a damn good one," Jason said.

My blood flowed a little faster. "What? Where'd you hear that?"

Dwayne smirked. "Oh honey. He's a bartender, and gays talk. Donny's got a *lot* to talk about, if you know what I mean."

Jason flopped his arm on the table with a loud

thunk and my two best friends broke into a fit. The redder my ears turned, the louder they laughed. Finally, salvation came in the form of a Flo's Diner waitress uniform.

Katie sidled up to our table. "Hon, are they badgering you again?"

"No, we're preparing him for an incoming torpedo," Jason gasped. Dwayne had tears running down both cheeks. I looked up, hoping Katie would save me.

"Don't let them get to you, sweetie." She leaned down and whispered loud enough for everyone to hear. "I assume your plumbing works the same as mine. Just lay back and relax—and whatever you do, *don't clench.*"

My jaw dropped.

Jason howled, and Dwayne, having lost any semblance of composure, was horizontal.

Katie, *my salvation,* made a dramatic gesture and a popping noise with one palm hitting the side of her other fist, then walked away laughing.

19

HOW CATS DO IT

Three dinner dates and four bar visits later, I'd still not see Donny's naked glory. If it hadn't been for Jason's ribbing, I might not have thought much about it, but now it nagged at me. I dreamed scenes of walking into an empty bar, of Donny stripping and taking me on the counter where Dwayne's limes usually sat. The little devil had evicted the angel completely and was practically stroking me into an overheated state day and night. I guess I could've turned to AOL—or to more *handy* methods—but I wanted Donny.

We'd been dating six weeks. Hell, in gay years that's practically a silver anniversary. Shouldn't he get me a punch bowl or something?

And it wasn't just that I was horny. I was starting to doubt myself. Maybe he wasn't interested in me *that* way. Maybe he didn't want to get naked. I knew I was filling out my clothes nicely now. Other guys confirmed that when they eye-licked me across the bar.

Yes, eye-licking is a thing, and it feels good to be the lickee. It's very flattering.

I hated having so many questions and doubts. They were silly. I knew it. Donny liked me, and we made out like champs. He wouldn't do that with someone he wasn't interested in, would he? Of course not. I just needed to be patient and ride this out.

Shit. I said *ride*.

Now I was horny again.

I pulled into—

Damn it, everything sounds sexual now.

I *parked* in his driveway for a planned Thursday night dinner and playdate with the pack. Donny was down to just the cougars, as Roxy had outgrown the hand-raising stage and was firmly ensconced in her new home at the zoo. It was crazy how quickly the chipmunks had grown, and Donny now used rubber nubs on their claws to keep from accidental piercings. Despite their increased size, they were still as cute as ever, and far cleverer. We played, then I fed them while Donny finished cooking dinner. The little beasts would start solid food soon, so I wanted to enjoy as much bottle time as possible.

After a dinner of pot roast and veggies—a ridiculously delicious meal, by the way—we retired to the den and snuggled on the couch. During a commercial break, Donny leaned down and kissed me. A peck grew into a kiss, then a passionate tongue-probing make-out session. We never returned to the show.

The devil stabbed me with his pitchfork, so I decided to try something. Ever so hesitantly, I reached up and began unbuttoning Donny's shirt. I got two undone before he realized what was happening and placed his hand over mine, stopping my dastardly deed in its tracks.

I looked up, a question in my eyes.

He sighed, and his eyes fell. When he spoke, his voice was quiet. "Can we wait?"

My brow crinkled. "Of course. There's no rush. I just thought—"

"I know it's probably weird that we haven't done anything more than kiss yet." His eyes flitted from mine to the floor and back. "I guess I'm paranoid about being a bartender."

Huh? I wasn't sure what reason I expected, but it wasn't that.

He must've seen the confusion, so he continued. "Everybody thinks we sleep around all the time. I work in a bar where a lot of guys go just to hook up. I mean, we do get hit on a lot. Plenty of the staff gets more than their share of sex. The reputation is probably well-earned. I leave work most nights with at least one phone number in my pocket, usually more than one. But it's not a glamorous life. By the time the bar closes and we clean up, it's three or four in the morning. We're too exhausted to hook up with anybody—and those phone numbers end up in the trash more often than not."

All those thoughts had crossed my mind when we'd first met. I'd assumed bartenders got tail pretty much every night. The thought of trusting someone so public, so sought after, made my skin crawl. Hearing him describe things from his perspective gave me pause. Had I misjudged bartenders? Clearly, I'd misjudged him, even if others acted differently.

He leaned against the arm of the couch, staring down at his hands. "I really like you—a lot. More than I've liked anybody in a long time."

He looked up, and he looked unsure or nervous, maybe even afraid. I wasn't sure, but I wanted to reach out somehow. "Donny, I feel the same. I've loved every minute we've spent together."

He smiled weakly. "I know. I get that. It's just… there's so much you don't know about me. You might not feel the same when you learn it all."

I fell back on the only thing I could think of: humor. "Did you kill someone?"

He chuckled. "No."

"How about rape or pillage? Maybe burn a village or two? You're not secretly a Viking, are you?"

His eyes rolled dramatically. "No, I'm not a Viking. No raping or pillaging."

"Oh! I know what it is. You don't have a penis and you're scared I won't like you without one."

He finally laughed. "No, that's *definitely* not it—and it works just fine, thank you very much."

"You're a bartender slut, sleeping with every old man who wiggles his wrinkles at you?"

He smacked my arm. "No! Never the wrinkles."

I cupped his cheek affectionately. "If it's none of those things, we'll face it together. I'm not scared of you or your furry family, mister."

"I hope so." He sobered and looked into my eyes. "I really hope so."

THAT NIGHT, I STAYED AT HIS PLACE FOR THE FIRST time. I slept with his arms wrapped around me, the rise and fall of his chest lulling me to sleep. I usually slept naked, but that night I wore shorts and a T-shirt.

You just did that to spite him. If you couldn't see his Klondike bar, he couldn't see yours, the little devil jeered in my mind—but he was wrong.

Donny's honesty, even his insecurity and vulnerability, somehow made me like him more. The Pisces in me needed to take care of someone, and here was a man who desperately needed support.

Sign me up, coach!

I woke the next morning with Donny staring down at me. His head was propped on one elbow while his other hand gently stroked my hair. In that moment, in that one look, any doubts I had about his feelings for me vanished. This was a man who guarded his heart—but when he cared, he cared deeply, with everything he had.

For whatever reason, his heart was opening *to me*.

Was I worthy of it?

I watched him watch me, and neither of us spoke. I studied his face, the curve of his nose, the line of his jaw. My eyes traced the tiny creases forming around his eyes. There was a quiet strength to this man. Yes, there was pain hidden deep within him, I could see that in the depth of his gaze, but there was also joy and love.

A smile tugged at the corners of my mouth.

"What?" he asked.

"You feel good."

His manly face transformed into a boyish grin.

"And I don't just mean your body next to mine.

Waking up and seeing you before anything else…Donny—"

He pressed his forefinger to my lips, then leaned down and replaced it with his mouth.

I melted into his arms, and visions of rose petals and doves fluttered, unbidden, through my mind. I tried to giggle at my silliness, but his tongue stifled my mirth. Strong hands gripped my back and pressed me into him. His warmth filled me with a joy I'd thought lost.

Images of wings and roses returned.

This time I smiled and watched the petals as they drifted on the wind. They would land one day, and in that moment, I hoped with all my heart they'd land on the man beside me.

EPILOGUE

Nothing but the Truth

I know what you're thinking. Where's the sticky, steamy, sweaty romp with your protagonist's new man? Never fear, dear reader. There's plenty more where that came from . . . just not in the way you might expect.

Donny and I . . . well, let me just say this: our sexcapades didn't exactly follow the script.

But that's a story for another day. Prepare yourself, it's quite the ride.

And yes, I said *ride*. Stop it, you naughty sausage.

Get your copy of My Dream Date to continue Michael's (my) journey.

BOOKS BY CASEY MORALES

Raised by Wolves series

My Accidental First Date

My Next Date

My Wildest Date

My Dream Date

My Last Date